THE SQUAMPKIN PATCH

A NASSELROGT ADVENTURE

JT PETTY

Illustrated by David Michael Friend

Simon & Schuster Books for Young Readers
New York London Toronto Sydney

SIMON & SCHUSTER BOOKS FOR YOUNG READERS

An imprint of Simon & Schuster Children's Publishing Division

1230 Avenue of the Americas, New York, New York 10020

SIMON & SCHUSTER BOOKS FOR YOUNG READERS is a trademark of Simon & Schuster, Inc.

Book design by Einav Aviran

The text for this book is set in Adobe Garamond.

The illustrations for this book are rendered in ink.

Manufactured in the United States of America

2 4 6 8 10 9 7 5 3 1

Library of Congress Cataloging-in-Publication Data

Petty, J. T. (John T.)

The squampkin patch : a Nasselrogt adventure / J.T. Petty.—1st ed.

p. cm.

Summary: After escaping from the Urchin House Orphanage, Milton, age eleven, and his sister Chloe, age eight, settle into the empty house of a candy maker where they encounter a very sinister pumpkin patch. Includes a recipe for pumpkin chocolate chip cookies.

ISBN-13: 978-1-4169-0274-4

ISBN-10: 1-4169-0274-0

[1. Pumpkin—Fiction. 2. Candy—Fiction. 3. Brothers and sisters—Fiction.] I. Title.

PZ7.P448139Squ 2006

[Fic]—dc22

2005019783

FIRST
EDITION

For Dad, who warned about the monsters in the basement.

Acknowledgments

Many thanks to Lizz Zitron and my sister, Kate, who were the first to read this book. Kate taught me the song, "Melancholy Baby." Lizz provided great friendship and a library of cookbooks. Both gave invaluable editorial advice. Thanks to Faye Bender, David Gale, and Alexandra Cooper. Thanks to M&R Ake, Inc., for the use of their logo. And thanks to my parents, who let me eat more candy than any child should, or most children could.

To the Reader

"Nasselrogt" is pronounced "Nasal Rod." This is not as difficult as, say, performing dentistry on an unanesthetized bear, or tying your shoe with one hand. But for teachers, waiting-room attendants, roll callers, and countless others, the pronunciation of Nasselrogt was an insurmountable peak.

For years, Milton and Chloe Nasselrogt had stoically suffered hearing their name pronounced as if the speaker were trying to cough up an angry kitten. In a world of unlikely names, the many ways Nasselrogt was literally spat out was usually a minor annoyance, and often funny, if sometimes a little damp.

But in the eleventh year of Milton's life and the eighth year of Chloe's, the mispronunciation of the name they had inherited from their parents would be the snag by which those parents were lost.

Chapter 1

Duck in the Pants

A rack of trousers, a pair of tanning beds, and their own last name conspired to orphan the Nasselrogt children.

After the Great Cheese Grater Fiasco, the Nuked Alaska Ice Cream Debacle, and the Taffy Handkerchief Catastrophe, Milton and Chloe were all out of nannies. So Mr. and Ms. Nasselrogt, despite their busy schedules, had been forced to take their children back-to-school shopping themselves.

Off went the Nasselrogt Four to the mall.

"Can we get extra books?" Chloe asked.

"I'll need a flamethrower for geography class," Milton said. He was much less excited than Chloe about their return to school.

Mr. and Ms. Nasselrogt were enormously skilled at ignoring their children. Ms. Nasselrogt was incapable of hanging up the mobile telephone that connected her to the office. Mr. Nasselrogt loved buying things for Mr. Nasselrogt.

"There's no 'idle' in 'middle management,'" said Ms. Nasselrogt to her mobile phone.

"Look at the size of this barbecue!" said Mr. Nasselrogt.

"There's only one 'd' in 'idle,'" said Ms. Nasselrogt.

"How many blenders do we have?" said Mr. Nasselrogt.

Ms. Nasselrogt ignored him, saying into her phone, "That's why there's a 'nag' in 'management.'"

"Mom, Dad? Milton just . . ." Chloe let the sentence trail off; both of her parents were ignoring her.

"No, not like a horse, like a busybody," her mom said to the phone.

"Oooooh, tanning beds! It says they've got 'scream buffers'!" Mr. Nasselrogt said.

"Hold on." Ms. Nasselrogt put her hand over the phone's mouthpiece to be polite, and asked her husband, "Did we get Milton's school socks yet?"

"Nope, his ankles were too chubby. I think the Hefty Boy Socks section is over there," Mr. Nasselrogt said, looking into the buffed metallic dome of the tanning bed, regarding a reflection that suddenly seemed too pale.

"Where *is* Milton?" Ms. Nasselrogt asked.

But Milton had already gone into the pants. Ignored by his parents, and unable to face the shame of shopping in the Hefty Boy Socks section, Milton had ducked into a circular rack of trousers. He crouched in the dim hollow at its center, suddenly alone and safe from the mall.

"Where's Chloe?" Mr. Nasselrogt asked.

Chloe, by whom nothing escaped unnoticed, had caught her brother wiggling his ears, a dead giveaway that he was contemplating an entertaining bit of misbehavior. She had watched him duck in the pants when their parents' backs were turned.

Milton yelped like an electrocuted seal when Chloe's head poked into his trouser fort. He would not admit to Chloe that chubby ankles were the cause of his flight, but she had already figured it out on her own.

"Maybe they'll forget about socks," said Chloe.

"This *is* my hiding place," said Milton. "Why couldn't you find your own?"

"Milton?" said Ms. Nasselrogt from outside the trousers, before Chloe could answer.

Milton put a finger to his lips.

They crouched in their corduroy igloo, a little giddy at their own daring.

"Milton!" called out Ms. Nasselrogt.

"Chloe!" called out Mr. Nasselrogt.

Milton and Chloe had often felt nearly invisible in their parents' eyes, no matter what they did. Now they felt completely invisible, and by their own doing. They looked at each other and smiled, stifling giggles.

"Milton! Chloe!"

"They must be close," said Ms. Nasselrogt.

"Do you think I'm too pale?" asked Mr. Nasselrogt.

And then they were silent.

When Milton and Chloe emerged from the trouser rack, their parents were gone.

They searched, increasingly nervous, but their parents were nowhere to be seen. Milton searched the Pajamas section. Chloe searched Housewares. Milton stumbled through Ladies' Intimates, covering his eyes for modesty's sake as he groped desperately for his mom and dad. (He found something silky that shrieked and slapped him, but no sign of his parents.)

When they realized they couldn't see each other, Milton and Chloe called out and followed the sound of each other's voice until they were together.

"Why are you crying? Stop it," Milton said.

"I wasn't crying," Chloe said, wiping at her damp cheeks. When Milton realized they were standing hand-in-hand, he jerked his mitts back and hid them in his pockets.

Their parents were gone.

Every pair of adults they saw made their hearts leap with hope. Every revelation that it was another pair of strangers made their hearts splat with despair.

It took them twenty minutes to teach the security guard how to pronounce "Nasal Rod." She called out over the intercom for half an hour before management complained that it was interrupting the Muzak.

The security guard gave them lollipops and a few dollars for bus fare.

Milton and Chloe went into the parking lot and waited by the family car until dusk, then walked to the bus stop and went home.

They were latchkey kids, and almost never returned home to find their parents there waiting. They fed themselves dinner, Milton including a course of cookies both before and after their microwaved macaroni and cheese.

Milton tried calling his parents' mobile phones a dozen times each. He quickly realized that they would not answer, but hearing the sounds of their recorded voicemail messages was, at least, some small comfort.

Then they went to their rooms, crawled into their beds, and fell asleep hoping they would be awakened by their mom and dad.

No such luck.

Milton called the police, who raced over, broke down the door, and held the Nasselrogt children at gunpoint until they realized that they had mixed up the addresses. (Across town, a hostage crisis was averted when a social worker showed up with a plate of cookies and hugs.)

Milton and Chloe spent the afternoon at the police station.

They had no surviving family members, their parents had no close friends, and the police would not allow them to spend another night alone in their home.

So the Nasselrogt children were taken to Urchin House, an orphanage where they made the unfortunate acquaintance of Mr. Porifera.

Chapter 2

Khaki Mayo

Mr. Yon Kinsky Kozinsky Porifera's desk was so shiny that his upside-down reflection was as sharp and bright as the man himself. In its polished surface, Milton could see right up Mr. Porifera's enormous nostrils, almost to his brain. Milton could not, however, see what Mr. Porifera was thinking, unless he was thinking of nose dirt.

"Welcome to Urchin House," Porifera said in a voice neat and clipped, like a miserable poodle. His ever-exposed front teeth smacked dryly against his lower lip.

He read Milton's and Chloe's files. Porifera loved files.

"Chloe and Milton . . . Nassss . . . Nessss . . . Neck . . ." he said.

"It's pronounced 'Nasal Rod,'" said Chloe, quietly.

Porifera hated being corrected. Especially by children. He placed Chloe's and Milton's files in the "TROUBLE" section of his filing cabinet.

"Well, aren't you a clever child," said Porifera. This was true:

Chloe was a very clever child. Nonetheless, she rarely spoke, even though she knew big words like "dextrorotatory"[1] and "levorotatory."[2]

Urchin House was far from town, in the middle of an enormous parking lot in the middle of an enormous prairie. The front half was white columns and gables; the back half was gray warehouses and smokestacks. It did not look like the marriage of a factory and an orphanage. It looked like a factory had tried to swallow an orphanage, choked, and died with its mouth full.

Milton and Chloe were given uniforms, toothbrushes, a slice of a loaf of something brown that squeaked when poked with a fork and answered to the name of dinner, and then sent to bed.

Five hours later, before the sun could muster the will to rise, the Nasselrogt children were awoken and sent to work in the zipper factory.

With the other unfortunate orphans, they spent long hours gluing zipper teeth one by one onto strips of plasticky fabric. The great ring of keys hanging from Porifera's belt jingled like spurs as he paced the length of the assembly line.

Chloe watched the other children. Nobody but she and Milton ever looked up from their work. The oldest children operated

---

1 A big word for "turning clockwise." For example, you could say, "The Horologist used an almagest and the dextrorotatory perambulations of his chronometer to determine his longitude by means of celestial navigation."

2 A big word for "turning counter-clockwise."

the ovens where plastic was melted down and shaped into teeth. Chloe watched the noxious black fumes rise from the plastic and hover before it was whisked away into the smokestacks by enormous fans.

Breakfast brown-loaf came with brown ketchup. Lunch brown-loaf came with brown mustard. Dinner brown-loaf came with mayonnaise. The mayonnaise was khaki.

"This is awful," said Milton.

Mr. Porifera smiled at him without humor and drew a pinched thumb and forefinger across his lips: Zip it!

Back in the shopping mall, on the outskirts of the department store's Hefty Boy section, the security guard found a mobile telephone lying between two tanning beds.

Looking down at her reflection in one of the bed's silver domes, it occurred to the guard that both beds had been sealed for several days. She pressed the release clasps, and the two tanning beds yawned like waking oysters in which swine had been cast as pearls. For inside, two enormous hams had been roasted to a rich orange.

One of the hams opened its eyes and yelled, "Milton!"

The other ham sprang up and yelled, "Chloe!"

The security guard swallowed her lollipop, stick and all. Mr. and Ms. Nasselrogt leaped to their feet and ran toward the exit.

"Milton! Chloe!" they shouted.

On the way to their car, Ms. Nasselrogt accidentally knocked over an old man who would later file a police report stating that he had been viciously attacked by two gigantic peeled sweet potatoes.

Milton poked his dinner loaf with a fork.

"Squeak!" it said.

He looked up and down the cafeteria bench where he was perched. All of the dozens of other boys there had enormous eyes and tiny mouths, into which they dutifully pushed dinner brownloaf and khaki mayo. "Squeak! Squeak!" said their dinners. The boys said nothing at all.

"How long have you been here?" Milton whispered to the boy at his side.

"I make zippers," the boy said, never lifting his eyes from his plate.

I need to get out of here, thought Milton, not for the first time.

Chloe, brushing her teeth with the other girls, was nursing the same thought.

"How did your parents die?" asked the girl to her left.

"My parents aren't dead," said Chloe.

"Oooh," said the girl on her right, "then they must not want you."

Chloe froze, toothpaste foam ringing her mouth. This had not occurred to her.

Mr. and Ms. Nasselrogt, finding no sign of their children at home, called the police.

The police arrived and held them at gunpoint until the Nasselrogts convinced them that they were human beings, and not the peeled-sweet-potato mutants reported to be terrorizing the elderly.

"We had a tanning accident," said Mr. Nasselrogt.

"Understood," said a blond cop named Orson, making his solitary appearance in this story. "I like tanning. It makes you look healthy."

"We need to find our children," said Ms. Nasselrogt.

At the police station, the Nasselrogts were told that their children had been sent to an orphanage called Urchin House.

Porifera's telephone pulled him out of a dream in which he had improved the Dewey Decimal System to such an extent that they were going to call it the Porifera Point Paradigm. It was a very sweet dream, and he resented being awoken.

"Urchin House. Y. K. K. Porifera speaking," he said.

"You have our children," said Ms. Nasselrogt.

"I'm sorry?" said Porifera.

"Milton and Chloe Nasselrogt. I'm their mother, and—"

"Ah, I see," interrupted Porifera. "You are mistaken. You see, Urchin House is an orphanage. It's filled with orphans. And orphans, by definition, don't have mothers."

Ms. Nasselrogt would not give up, and pressed Porifera to look through his files. Stroking his filing cabinets lovingly, he condescended to check.

"'Nasal Rod' you said the name was?" he said.

"Yes, it's spelled—" But before Ms. Nasselrogt could finish, Porifera again interrupted.

"I'm an excellent speller, ma'am," he said, as his fingers, remarkably long for so short a man, flitted gracefully through the files.

"It's spelled N-A-S-S-E-L-R-O-G-T," said Ms. Nasselrogt.

Porifera, scanning through each section of his meticulously organized filing system, was not listening. He hated to be corrected, even by adults.

"I assure you, ma'am, there is no need to instruct my spelling, and there are no Nasal Rod children at Urchin House."

He hung up on Ms. Nasselrogt as she tried to protest.

The phone rang again immediately. Porifera unplugged it from the wall, so it would not further disturb his dreams.

Chapter 3

The Big Zipper

The boys and girls of Urchin House were filed away in bed. Milton lay on one of the top bunks, too preoccupied to sleep. The other boys' spirits seemed to have been broken by brown-loaf and zipper construction.

"Don't you want anything more than to make zippers?" he whispered to the boy on the bunk below. "Do you ever think of getting out of here?"

The boy, a scrawny specimen with enormous eyes and tiny teeth, nodded his head. A glint of passion sparked in one eye, the first hint of emotion Milton had detected among his fellows at the orphanage.

"I've been working on this," said the boy. He reached beneath his pillow and pulled out an eleven-foot-long zipper. The canary in Milton's coal mine keeled over and died.

"I named it Jeffrey Jr." said the boy, whose name was Jeffrey. He smiled with teeth even smaller than those on the zipper he had named for himself.

Milton sighed.

* * *

Chloe was watching things very carefully. She needed to find a way for her and Milton to escape.

All of the windows were barred. All of the doors were locked. The zipper factory slumbered; the conveyor belts and ventilation fans were still. She had heard dogs barking outside earlier, but now they were quiet.

In the silence, it was hard not to think about the girl who had said that Chloe's parents did not want her.

Mr. and Ms. Nasselrogt sat in the back of a police cruiser as it sped down the highway. They watched the car's flashers throw red-and-blue light far out into the surrounding prairie. They would not reach Urchin House for several hours at least.

Milton crept out of bed. He tied his shoelaces together and hung his shoes around his neck.

"That's not how you wear shoes," whispered Jeffrey.

"They would make too much noise on my feet," Milton answered.

"Too much noise for what?"

"For my escape. I'm getting out of here."

Jeffrey's eyes widened.

"Here," he said, "you'll need this."

Jeffrey reached under his pillow and pulled out Jeffrey Jr., the eleven-foot-long zipper.

Milton was touched, even if Jeffrey was obviously a little sugar short of peanut brittle. Jeffrey nodded encouragingly and held out the zipper. Milton took it.

"Chloe," Milton whispered.

Chloe jumped softly out of bed, ready. Milton did not even have to tell her they were making an escape.

"That's a big zipper," she said.

The first door Milton tried was locked.

"They're *all* locked," said Chloe, quietly. "This way."

She tiptoed to the zipper factory, and Milton followed.

The ventilation fans beneath the smokestacks were still. They could just fit between the blades, and, with Chloe in the lead, began to shimmy up the inside of one tall, narrow stack.

Looking past his sister, Milton could see moonlight at the top, six stories above them. Black grime rubbed off the bricks and covered them from head to toe.

As they climbed, the chimney grew narrower. Inching upward, Chloe began to imagine what would happen if she got stuck. She pictured herself wedged inside the narrow tunnel of bricks, arms pinned at her sides, able to take only the smallest breaths. She felt the bricks pressing in on her, closer and closer. It felt as if she were trapped in the coils of a great brick-and-mortar boa constrictor.

Below, Milton could hear Chloe's breath quickening.

Poop in a bag and pop it, he thought. *This is not good.*

"Chloe," he whispered, "this is not the time to get cluster . . . cloister . . . what's the word?"

"Claustrophobic," she said, barely breathing. She had been terrified of small spaces for as long as she could remember.

Within arm's reach of the chimney's top, Chloe froze. Milton's head bumped into her feet.

"Holy mackerel, Chloe," he said. "We're almost there. Keep going."

Chloe could not move. She imagined the bricks were giant molars that were slowly grinding her between them.

"Move, Chloe!" Milton said. "I'd leave you here, but you're blocking the way." Chloe was frozen in place.

Milton, grimy and exhausted from the climb, and claiming a brother's natural-born right to no small amount of cruelty, began to tickle the soles of Chloe's bare feet. Electric eels could not have chased her out of the chimney as quickly.

She shot out of the top of the smokestack, several hundred feet above the hard, slate roof of Urchin House, shaking uncontrollably with laughter and scrabbling for purchase on the chimney's rim. Milton popped out after her.

Heights were no problem for either of the Nasselrogt children, and they quickly scurried down to the roof, then dropped to the ground.

As soon as their feet touched earth, a chorus of angry barks erupted from the night.

Porifera's office light came on.

"Run!" hissed Milton. No tickling was required this time to get Chloe in motion.

They flew across the parking lot, ignoring the pokes and jabs of asphalt pebbles against their bare feet. Windows blinked into life behind them. The baying grew louder as the hounds drew closer.

Milton glanced backward, and caught a glimpse of the first of the dogs rounding the corner of Urchin House. It was little more than a dark shape, but for its teeth, which glowed in the moonlight behind the hound's fogged breath.

Chloe began to drag behind, hopping a little to favor the foot with a pebble wedged painfully between her toes.

An entire pack of dogs rounded the corner behind the one in the lead, nearly a dozen sets of gleaming teeth dancing in the darkness, drawing closer.

Milton grabbed Chloe's hand and dragged her along, their bare feet slapping against the asphalt.

"Wall," said Chloe.

Milton squinted into the night ahead. There was a strip of absolute darkness covering the horizon. The strip grew until it loomed over them, and Milton and Chloe skidded to a stop inches from a twelve-foot-high brick wall.

"Oh," said Milton. "A wall."

The Nasselrogt children turned and looked at the hounds, halfway across the parking lot and steaming mercilessly toward them. They were close enough now to make out individual teeth in jaws that snapped at the air in eager anticipation. Like zippers opening and refastening in the night.

There's an idea, thought Milton. He pulled Jeffrey Jr. out of his uniform.

Chloe could not take her eyes off of the approaching hounds. She hoped the inside of a dog's stomach would not be too claustrophobic.

Milton turned to the wall and held Jeffrey Jr. by its fastener, letting the zipper hang its full length. He pressed the zipper against the wall, and made sure it stuck fast.

The dogs were nearly on them, the smell of the children's fear driving them to new heights of frenzy.

Milton unzipped the wall.

He grabbed Chloe's hand, pulled her through to the other side, then turned and zipped it back up again.

Thumpthumpthumpthumpthump! they heard as the pack of hounds barreled into the bricks.

Chloe breathed for the first time in half a minute. Milton whooped for joy.

Porifera wrung his hands together, pacing, muttering.

The orphans were assembled on the factory floor before him in rows.

"Who were they?" Porifera demanded once more.

The orphans were silent. The catatonia that so often pleased him was now a sore tooth in Porifera's mouthful of problems.

"Please," he said, "tell me the runaways' names. They are my—" he savored the word—"responsibility."

No answers from the orphans. Porifera sighed.

"Everybody loses condiment privileges until somebody tells me their names."

A stirring among the orphans. Their brown-loaf would be unbearable without its ketchup, mustard, or mayonnaise. Finally, Jeffrey stepped forward.

"It was the Nasselrogts, sir."

"The . . . Nasal Rods?" asked Porifera. The telephone conversation of several hours earlier returned like a poorly digested meal.

"Milton Nasselrogt," said Jeffrey.

"And Chloe Nasselrogt," added one of the girls.

When Yon Kinsky Kozinsky Porifera was still a boy, the other children would mock his name, and then make fun of him for crying so easily by saying "Poor Porifera" and pretending to play invisible violins.

Now, so many decades later, he thought to himself, *Poor Porifera.*

Milton had not been able to retrieve Jeffrey Jr., as it was now stuck on the far side of the wall.

The Nasselrogt children barely took the time to tie their shoes before starting out across the prairie. They needed to get as far as possible from Urchin House and Porifera before dawn.

They stayed close to the road, walking through the tall grass, counting on the grime from the smokestacks to keep them hidden.

Chloe saw the flashing red-and-blue lights first. Undoubtedly, Porifera had called the police.

Milton and Chloe pushed back farther into the grass, away from the road, and lay down where they hoped they could not be seen.

Milton and Chloe's mom gazed out of the window of the police car, watching the red-and-blue lights sweep over the miles of grass beyond the edge of the road. The panic at the loss of her children had been worn by a sleepless night into a deep weariness, and a desperate need to see them again.

Mr. Nasselrogt took her hand and squeezed it. They could see Urchin House up ahead.

Ms. Nasselrogt let her eyes wander back out over the prairie.

Her heart swelled at the sight of shapes in the grass, two bumps barely visible in the first rays of dawn.

But she was certain that it was only her eyes seeing what her mind so desperately wanted them to find. The shapes in the grass were black as chimney soot—probably old tires or garbage bags.

She leaned against Mr. Nasselrogt and closed her eyes.

Milton and Chloe waited until the police car had passed through the gates of Urchin House, and then continued down the road.

Shortly after the sun rose, they crossed a small stream in which they washed off as much of the chimney grime as they could. Without soap, however, they still kind of looked like old tires.

At a crossroads, knowing neither where they were nor which way was home, they decided to head in the direction most directly opposite that of Urchin House.

A bus approached, and Milton showed enough leg to convince it to stop.

The woman behind the wheel looked over the dirty children.

"You kids going to Goodfellow's Landing?" she asked.

"Is that where this bus goes?" asked Milton.

"Ayup," she said, which meant "Yes."

"Then that's where we're going," said Milton.

The bus driver squinted at Milton and Chloe, suspicious.

"You ain't runaway minors, are you?" she asked.

"No," said Chloe.

"Then why're you so dirty?"

Chloe looked at Milton.

"We're . . . miners," said Milton.

"That's a different story, then. My daddy was a miner. Always room for coal hounds on this bus."

She pressed a big green button on the bus's dashboard. The bus hissed mightily, hunkering down over its tires like a tired dog, lowering so that Milton and Chloe could step easily onto the stairs.

"Pneumatics," the bus driver said, with obvious satisfaction.

She used the pneumatics to raise the bus again and then welcomed the Nasselrogt children aboard, even letting Milton have some of the creamy, hummingbird-sweet coffee from her thermos. He hummed all the way to Goodfellow's Landing.

The Nasselrogt children's escape was a blessing in disguise for Porifera.

Their orange-colored parents had searched the orphanage up and down, storming around and interrupting an entire day's worth of zipper production. If they had found even the faintest trace of Milton or Chloe, they would have had proof of Porifera's filing error—more than enough reason for him to lose his job.

It was with great relief that he ushered them, teary-eyed and exhausted, out of Urchin House at day's end.

But settling down before his brown-loaf dinner, a thought began to nibble at the back of his brain. If the Nasselrogt children returned home, he would be blamed not only for the filing error, but also for the children's escape.

He tried to drown the thought in the squeaking of his dinner, but to no avail.

The threat loomed behind him in the bathroom mirror as he brushed his teeth before bed. The threat lay on the pillow by his head.

Porifera dreamt about opening the drawer of his filing cabinet to discover the Nasselrogt children curled inside, chewing up and swallowing the last of his files.

After breakfast the next morning, he wiped the brown ketchup from his lips and pulled on his traveling galoshes. He had to get the Nasselrogt children back in his zipper factory, and make sure they never, ever left.

THE SQUAMPKIN PATCH

Chapter 4

Tadpoles Splatting to Their Doom

There was a rumbling in the air like a hundred heavenly bowling balls. Chloe watched dark clouds boil above the drowsy little burg of Goodfellow's Landing.

At the depot, the bus driver bought them a late lunch of pimento-cheese sandwiches and grape soda, and asked them about their lives in the coal mines.

"Oh, you know," said Milton. "Pretty dark. Pretty . . . coaly." Chloe raised her eyebrows at Milton, an expression that left a stick-figure seagull creased into her forehead.

"Ayup. My dear daddy, may he finally find peace in the ground he dug, whiled away many a night with tales of the coaly below." The bus driver finished emptying the sugar silo into her thermos of coffee.

"Well. I gotta dock that old bus. It was a pleasure to meet you both. I'm Beulah." The bus driver reached out a hand to Milton.

"I'm Milton," he said, shaking her hand.

"Chloe," said Chloe, shaking the offered hand in turn.

* * *

They washed off the rest of the chimney grime in the depot bathrooms, then went to the ticket counter to find a bus home.

CLOSED UNTIL MONDAY read the sign at the empty counter.

"What day is today?" asked Milton.

"Saturday," Chloe said.

The town of Goodfellow's Landing was the kind of place that grows to resent the label "quaint" only because it fits so well.

Main Street was like Alan Ladd, short but handsome. There was a hardware store, a supermarket, and a thrift shop, but they were all closed.

"Do you think those boys would know a place we could stay?" asked Chloe.

"Who?"

"Those twins." Chloe pointed down the street, where a pair of twins was hurrying away.

"Oh, you mean those *girls*," Milton said.

Looking together, neither Milton nor Chloe could figure out who was right. The twins could just as easily have been boys *or* girls. Or possums, for that matter, so pinched and malicious were their faces. The Nasselrogts decided to carry on.

The sky was darkening, and Milton and Chloe picked up their pace. They soon found themselves out of town, walking past rural houses and lawns.

The outskirts of Goodfellow's Landing had the feeling of a village, with small wooden homes widely spaced on land that still held a few crops. Small businesses were mixed in among the homes—a vegetable market, a barbershop, a gas station.

Thick, heavy clouds spread like pancake batter over the afternoon sky. A strong wind was whipping the autumn leaves off the trees. A storm was coming.

They hurried down the street, hoping to find a place to stay before the storm broke. Raindrops fell, as fat as tadpoles, splatting to their doom against the asphalt.

"Let's build a teepee," said Milton.

"Let's knock on somebody's door," said Chloe. Sheet lightning flashed across the sky, illuminating the mountains of cloud above them.

Milton looked around.

In the avocado-green house before them, a dark figure was standing in the front window.

"Somebody's there," said Milton.

"Is he watching us?" asked Chloe.

"I don't know."

"Let's not find out."

Milton turned and looked at the bakery on the corner behind them. It was a small white box of a building, with ARGYLE CONFECTIONS painted on the dusty glass storefront, and inside, a row of empty display cases. Two handwritten signs were taped to the door, one reading BENNY NOT WELCOME, and the other, OUT TO LUNCH.

Chloe wondered whether Benny was not allowed inside, or if he was not invited to lunch.

Milton and Chloe cupped their hands against the glass and peered into the dark shop. It was utterly empty except for a few fossilized buns, shards of glass from the broken display cases, and a thick carpet of dust.

"He must have taken a long lunch," said Milton.

"What about there?" Chloe said, pointing to the large, white Victorian house behind the bakery. It waited well off the street, across a gnarly field of thick, woody vines.

As the rain began to fall more heavily, the Nasselrogt children ran toward the house, hopping through the tangle. The curling vines were somehow sinister, clutching at their ankles like dead, broken fingers.

"Pumpkins," said Chloe.

"What?" Milton asked, polka-dotted with rain.

"It's a pumpkin patch," she said, as they cleared the vines and ran up onto the house's porch. Chloe was close, but wrong. Much would happen before she discovered how terribly wrong she was.[3]

---

3 But to avoid confusion, and because I'm so comfortable lying to my readers, I'll just keep calling it a pumpkin patch.

Chapter 5

The Missing Argyle

There was no answer to Milton's knocks on the door. The rain was no longer just falling in sheets, but in quilts, in thick duvets—in whole beds.

Exhausted, Milton and Chloe sat on the porch and watched it fall.

"I don't think anybody's home," said Milton.

Chloe nodded, but didn't answer. She was already close to sleep. Several moments passed before she spoke.

"Milton? Where do you think Mom and Dad are?"

"I don't know," he said.

Chloe lay back on the porch and closed her eyes.

"A girl at the orphanage said that either they were dead, or they don't want us."

"No, no," said Milton. "It's probably just . . ."

But he couldn't think of a good explanation.

"What does some girl at an orphanage know, anyway?" he said.

"What it's like to be an orphan," said Chloe. She was not crying.

They slept on the porch, the sounds of summer's last storm roaring all around them.

The roar of the night's rain had ended.

Water seeped into the earth beneath the pumpkin patch. Inside their dreams, the Nasselrogt children heard a grumbling underground, a shifting of soil, as if something were waking up. . . .

Milton woke to the grumbling of his own stomach. It was the next morning, and he was hungry.

"Milton?"

He looked up. Chloe was standing on the threshold of the house, with her hand on the knob of the slightly opened door.

"It wasn't locked," she said.

Milton tried pushing on the door but something was holding it shut. He opened it enough to poke his head around the edge and saw a great pile of unopened mail leaning against the far side.

"There's nobody home." Milton grinned.

Inside the house, Milton shut the door behind them as Chloe examined a piece of mail.

"Charles Argyle," she said. "That's whose house this is."

"Like the bakery," said Milton. "Mr. Argyle?" he shouted. "Are you home? Mr. Argyle!"

They began to explore the house.

Milton ran through it frenetically, seeing everything at once and very little of any of it. Chloe's slower investigation did not take her far, but revealed much about the details.

The Argyle house had two stories, plus an attic and a basement. From the attic, Milton could see most of Goodfellow's Landing, and he had an excellent view of the pumpkin patch below. In the window of the avocado-green house across the street stood the figure of a man, still watching.

Chloe found an empty, torn-open envelope from someplace called M & R Ake, Inc., marked UNBEARABLY URGENT. Its logo was a row of identical figures with light-socket eyes. It looked like this:

On the second floor, Milton found the only bedroom—Charlie Argyle's. The bed made for excellent jumping, but it smelled funny. Stuck to the walls were pictures of France, and pages torn from real estate magazines showing Parisian pastry shops. Books and magazines filled with pictures of cookies, candies, and cakes littered the floor. Skimming the covers only made Milton hungry, so he continued his search elsewhere.

Downstairs, however, Chloe read carefully through one such magazine, a publication called *Perfectionist Confectioneering*. "Confectioneering" was the art of making candy.

"I think Charles Argyle is a candy maker," said Chloe to Milton, as he barreled down the stairs and into the living room.

"Whatever he was, he's gone," said Milton. In the living room, he found a television that did not work, and a sofa that made for merely decent jumping.

Chloe opened the dark, heavy door to the basement. A little of the living room's daylight reached tentatively into the gloom below.

Milton leaped from the sofa and ran into the kitchen. The yellow linoleum floor was dark with wear, like a slab of spicy mustard. Milton had no time to notice the piles of books, mounds of dust, or ancient, inedible cupcakes on the counter. His stomach demanded immediate attention.

He ran to the fridge and flung it open. Inside, he found black-speckled eggs and carrots that had shriveled like the fingers of a dead witch. A carton of milk displayed a black-and-white picture of a chubby boy about Chloe's age, with the words HAVE YOU SEEN ME? written in bold below. It smelled as if the milk had turned from liquid to solid and back again, several times.

That odor was nothing, however, compared to the stink that belched from the freezer. It smelled like they had been feeding the great apes in the monkey house nothing but licorice for a week, then forgotten to clean the cage.

Milton squinted into the dim interior. There was a dark, humanoid outline on the ridged floor of the freezer, like the shadow of a child. It looked like something baby-shaped had burnt there.

Milton stopped breathing for a moment, and not entirely because of the stench.

Yet even as he watched, the dark smudge faded and vanished.

Milton blinked, not even sure that he had ever seen the dark outline. He let the freezer door slowly shut.

A glimmer from the pantry caught his eye.

Still in the living room, Chloe peered into the darkness of the basement. Hundreds of white, glinting crescents winked at her from the darkness, lined neatly in rows. She squinted but could not identify the shapes. It almost felt like dozens of patient eyes, unblinking, watching her.

From the kitchen, her brother shrieked, as loud as the time he had tried to lick spilt molasses from an empty light fixture.

Chloe ran to the kitchen.

Behind her, the basement door slowly swung closed.

Milton was standing before a burlap sack of sugar that could easily have intimidated the greatest of sumo wrestlers, by stature or caloric content alone.

"It's beautiful," he whispered. The top of the sack gaped open, revealing snowy mounds of sugar. Morning light bounced off the tiny faceted crystals and danced over Milton's face.

"Grrrrrr," said Milton's stomach. He reached out to plunge his hand into the sugar. His fingers curled painfully against it, as if striking a rock.

"Ouch," said Milton.

The humidity in the air had solidified the mound of sugar into an unyielding boulder of sweetness.

"Grrrrrr!" said Milton's stomach again, frustrated.

Chloe had turned her attention to the rest of the room, which was as much library as kitchen. Her eyes sought out the dusty books and piles of paper stacked on every flat surface, all of them covered in hastily scribbled notes.

Open white bakery boxes on the countertop held long-fossilized cupcakes.

The cupboard over the sink, however, revealed dozens of boxes more. Chloe wasn't tall enough to reach, so she pointed them out to Milton.

He stopped licking the sugar boulder, walked over, and pulled down a box from the stack. It was filled with individually sealed candies. There were sugar-preserved kumquats with a crushed cashew coating, dark and milk chocolate almond clusters, three kinds of nougat, and chocolate-covered butter toffee.

"Breakfast!" said Milton.

Chapter 6

Milk Hammer Fall

They sat on the porch and each ate a box of candy, looking out over the pumpkin patch.

In the daylight, they could see how large the tangle of vines really was. It looked like an exhausted octopus that had missed its fainting couch. The gnarly vines sprawled across the front lawn and around the corner of the Argyle house, climbing the hill that rose almost to the height of the second floor.

On top of the hill, a great, twisted, box elder tree stretched toward the sky, taller than any telephone pole.

"Uh fink oo kin fee wiffle umkins," said Chloe, pointing at the dark-green nuggets the size of acorns clinging to the vines.

"What?" said Milton.

Chloe finished chewing her nougat and tried again. "I think those are little pumpkins."

Before Milton could respond, a woman who looked like a walrus wearing a sweatband and still angry about losing her tusks called out to them from the street.

"Why, hello there!" Her voice was so chipper it could have

made mulch; it did not match her narrow, suspicious eyes at all.

Milton and Chloe, mouths full of candy, waved.

The woman took the gesture as an invitation to join them on the porch, and began hopping across the vines of the pumpkin patch. Milton noticed that she had extraordinarily chubby ankles, and let a small, wicked coal of envy's opposite glow in his belly.

"You must be little Argyles," said the woman. "My name is Margery Milkhammer, but you can just call me Margery Milkhammer. Hahahahahahaha!" Her laughter sounded like a helicopter inhaling helium.

"I'm Milton," he said, "and this is Chloe."

"Well, aren't you two adorable? You'll have to meet my own children, they're probably about your age." Her eyes darted between them, sweeping over the details of their clothes, their hair, the dirt under their fingernails. "How old are your children?" asked Chloe.

"The same age," Margery said.

Milton and Chloe looked at her.

"They're thirteen years old," she continued. Then she whispered as if it were a secret, "They're twins."

Milton and Chloe nodded.

"Of course, they had to stay back a year, so you all might be in school together. Teacher thought they were cheating just because they always filled in the same answers."

Milton wished he was still eating candy, rather than talking to this woman. He looked downwards and saw that Margery was wearing ankle weights, and that her ankles were in fact quite slim.

"Dang," he said.

"Hmm?" Margery said. Milton played dumb. The woman tried again. "So you two must be little Argyles?"

Chloe shook her head.

"Little Nasselrogts," said Milton.

"Nasal . . . ?" Margery furrowed her brow.

"Rods," said Chloe.

"Oh. Nasselrogts. Then how do you know old Charlie?" Margery's eyes narrowed. Milton's ears wiggled.

"He's our uncle," he lied.

"Well, how do you like that," Margery said, not expecting an answer.

"Very much so," said Milton, providing one anyway.

"Is your Uncle Charlie back home? We haven't seen him in quite a while."

"Nope, it's just us," said Milton.

"Hmm? Just the two of you? I hope you're not as mysterious as your uncle. He was quite the topic of speculation." Margery swung her gaze around to focus on Chloe. Chloe jammed a fistful of nougat into her mouth so that she would not have to speak.

"Well, we sure do miss his confections. You know, he never told the neighborhood where he was going . . . ."

"That sounds like Uncle Charlie," said Milton.

"So where is he?" Margery asked.

Chloe chewed laboriously and looked at her brother, watching his ears wiggle and waiting for an answer.

"On holiday," Milton said.

"Holiday? For a whole year? Why, we haven't seen Charlie Argyle since . . . well, since last Halloween. That's an awfully long holiday."

"He really needed some relaxation," Milton said.

"Well, you can say that again. Bless his heart, but your uncle could be a might . . . testy sometimes. People started all sorts of rumors about the things he'd get up to inside this house. When my twins were smaller, they almost couldn't walk into his sweetshop they were so scared of him."

Chloe realized which twins she was speaking of, the possum-looking children they had seen the day before. She wanted to ask, *Are your children boys or girls?*

But instead she swallowed her nougat and said, "What are your children's names?"

"Brad and Erica," said Margery, her eyes losing their suspicious glint for a brief moment. "Maybe you could come over for a play-date next week?"

"Gosh, we'd love to," said Milton, adding fib number four to the conversation. "But we're leaving on the first bus Monday."

Chloe looked past Margery and at the avocado-green house across the street. The dark figure in the window was more difficult to see in the daylight, but he was still there, watching them.

She shielded her eyes and leaned around Milkhammer to get a better view. Chloe noticed a child's swing hanging from a tree in the front yard, its rusty chains testifying to months without use.

Chloe knew that the figure in the window was watching her. She could feel the weight of a strange gaze, almost like a pressure on her chest.

Chloe had been paying so little attention to the conversation that she did not even realize it had ended until Margery Milkhammer yipped like a small dog. Chloe looked over just in time to see her falling in the middle of the pumpkin patch.

She bounced back up like a whack-a-mole on the rebound and said, "Darn thing reached out and grabbed me!"

Chapter 7

Keep Away from Moisture

Supersaturated with sugar, the Nasselrogt children madly set up camp in the Argyle house. They were only staying until a Monday bus could take them home, but Milton reasoned that they might as well make themselves comfortable.

Neither wanted Charlie Argyle's bed, as it smelled of pumpernickel bread and soured milk. Milton called the sofa in the living room downstairs, and Chloe arranged a nest of blankets on the floor nearby.

They dragged all the rotten and dried-out food to the Dumpster behind Argyle's sweetshop, except for the sugar boulder, which Milton insisted they keep "just in case." Several times Chloe caught Milton either licking the boulder or whispering to it, and decided not to ask what he was doing for fear that he might tell her.

Forty-five minutes of hard work left them famished again, so they took a candy break, each consuming another boxful.

Chloe lay on the ground and held her stomach. Milton ran in a small circle until the sugar had cleared the place where his brain and spinal cord met, then decided to look around some more.

"I'm going to investigate Argyle's bakery," said Milton.

"Ooooooh," said Chloe, lying on the floor and holding her candy-sore belly.

Milton's path to Argyle Confections led through the gnarled heart of the pumpkin patch. He picked his way through it as carefully as he would have a stranger's nose.

He found the front door firmly sealed with a lock rusted well past any key's influence. The back door next to the Dumpster, was similarly impassable.

Behind the Dumpster, however, Milton found a rough hole torn in the wall of the shop, a broken ventilation cover lying nearby. The rim of the hole was ragged, as if the vent had been ripped out by raccoons or rats.

Lying on his belly, Milton was able to shimmy through the opening and pull himself into the bakery.

He was immediately covered in white dust, moldered pastry flour that puffed in clouds around him as he scrambled to his feet. The bakery's back room was even more of a disaster than the front.

Everything that was not bolted down had been strewn across the room, dented, or shattered. Mechanical mixers and confectioner's presses had been broken into pieces, their mechanical guts strewn. Every cabinet door was flung open, some hanging from a single hinge.

The bakery had been burgled. Overturned candy boxes and empty wrappers were everywhere. It looked as if an army of candy-starved children had ransacked the shop.

Every step Milton took kicked up another billowing cloud of flour. After several minutes' search of the shop revealed nothing but wreckage, he got tired of breathing the flour-filled air, and crawled back out into the pumpkin patch, powdered pale as any ghost.

Back in the house, Milton left white foot- and handprints around Charlie Argyle's bedroom as he rummaged through the absent owner's belongings.

Argyle's toothbrush had grown a bushy beard of mold around the bottom edge of its bristly, rectangular face; it kind of looked like Abraham Lincoln. His closet held seven pairs of identical baker's uniforms, hung neatly in a row. There were a dozen pairs of long underwear and a dozen pairs of green socks lying crumpled on the closet floor.

Beneath Argyle's bed, Milton discovered an old suitcase.

There were three things inside.

The first was a journal, filled nearly all the way through with tiny, obsessive handwriting. The cover read THE PUMPKIN/ CHOCOLATE TRIALS. Charles Argyle.

The second was a metal container, about the size of a cereal box, fastened securely with brass clasps on all four sides. One side was labeled SQUAMPKINS. Keep away from moisture. M & R AKE, INC.

The other side was labeled DANGER.

The third thing Milton found, held together with a red rubber band, was a fat stack of twenty-dollar bills.

Milton returned to the kitchen, where Chloe was recovering valiantly from a sugar-induced coma. He showed her the metal "squampkin" box, the journal, and the money.

Chloe picked up the box and shook it. Some lonely kernel rattled inside. She put the box on her lap and set about trying to pry off the lid.

"There's . . . thousands of dollars here," Milton said.

"Okay." Chloe did not seem so interested. Her tongue stuck out slightly from the corner of her mouth, as if hoping to help her discover how to unfasten the latches on the box.

"Here, let me try." Milton took the box out of her hands.

Chloe picked up the journal.

The first entry in the "Pumpkin/Chocolate Trials" was dated May 27, and it began, "Cinnamon can bridge pumpkin and chocolate. Maybe a touch of nutmeg. Maybe even ginger!"

Chloe flipped through the rest of the journal. Recipes, diary entries, and sketches were scattered throughout.

Milton's fingers were capable of untangling puzzles he could never have wrapped his brain around, and the ten clever digits made short work of the four intricate brass clasps that held the squampkin case shut.

The metal lid gave a faint *pop* and swung open, revealing the lonely kernel inside. It was similar to a pumpkin seed, but smaller, and dark red like cherry wood.

Chloe flipped to the back of the journal. A dozen or more pages had been ripped out, leaving only the last sheet. The final entry was a single line, hastily scrawled in Argyle's flyspeck script: "Helsabeck! He got to the patch before me! He must have sowed it with candy! His punishment . . ." The penned line trailed off, the sentence incomplete.

Milton pressed his finger against the squampkin seed and lifted it from the box. He held it a few inches from his face.

On the wider, rounded end, two small dimples, like eyes, were pressed into the hulled surface of the seed.

Chloe looked at the date of the last entry: October 31.

"Halloween," she said.

Milton looked up at her, and the seed fell from his finger.

"This is the last thing Argyle wrote before he disappeared."

The stack of twenty-dollar bills, however, had regained Milton's attention. He thought of his third grade math teacher's explanation of multiplication with grudging gratitude as he figured in his head that fifty of the bills would equal one thousand dollars. He began to count out stacks of fifty bills on the kitchen floor.

The autumn days were growing shorter, and in the shade of the box elder tree, the dusk-lit kitchen barely offered enough light to read by. Chloe flipped the light switch, but its heavy click had no effect on the darkly smudged bulb overhead.

"Do we have any candles?" she asked.

Milton shook his head, lips silently tracing numbers as he continued to count.

Chloe grabbed a box of matches from the stovetop, but could not find any candles. She eyed the solidified mound of sugar crouching in the pantry, and grabbed a knife. "Hey," Milton said, looking up from his counting. "You're not going to hurt my sugar boulder, are you?"

"I'm just chipping off a little piece, since we don't have any candles," Chloe said.

"Ah, right," said Milton. A year earlier, to the chagrin and loss of one of their last babysitters, Milton had discovered that sugar burned quite nicely.

Chloe chipped a chick-size chunk onto a china saucer. She set it on the ground next to Argyle's journal, lit a match, and set the sugar afire. The flame danced across the white crystalline surface, sometimes orange and sometimes blue, giving off a faint smell of toffee.

By its light, Chloe flipped back to the beginning of the "Pumpkin/Chocolate Trials" and began to read.

Chapter 8

The Pumpkin/Chocolate Trials,
May 27–June 8

May 27

Cinnamon can bridge pumpkin and chocolate. Maybe a touch of nutmeg. Maybe even ginger! A mature sweet, a spicy sweet. A cookie the grubby little worm-ball fingers of children will never touch!

Start simple. Canned pumpkin. Vegetable shortening replaces butter, combat the cakiness of pumpkin.

We begin—

PUMPKIN CHOCOLATE-CHIP COOKIES, 5.27

PREHEAT OVEN TO 375 DEGREES.

IN ONE BOWL, CREAM:
2 C. white sugar
1 C. shortening

ADD:
2 eggs

THEN:
16 oz. canned pumpkin
1 t. vanilla

IN ANOTHER BOWL, MIX:
4 C. white flour
1 t. baking powder
1 t. cinnamon
1/2 t. nutmeg
1/2 t. ginger

**COMBINE THE WET AND DRY
INGREDIENTS, THEN MIX IN:**
12 oz. bittersweet chocolate chips

**DROP ROUNDED TABLESPOONS ON AN
UNGREASED COOKIE SHEET, BAKE FOR
12 MINUTES.**

"Anything good?" Milton asked her, about halfway through his counting.

"Recipes, mostly," Chloe said. She flipped through several pages, past random scribblings until another entry seemed interesting.

> *May 29*
> Cakiness. Curse it! These aren't cookies. These are muffin caps. Where is my flake? Where is my crisp edge?
> Tried shortening instead of butter. Still cakey. Just a coarser crumb. Tried cutting the butter into the flour, like I was making pie dough. Still cakey! Canola oil a disaster. Absolute Hindenburg.
> I'm going to set Benny on fire.

And to illustrate the point, Charlie Argyle had drawn a crude cartoon of a round little boy labeled BENNY peeking out of an oven.

> *May 30*
> I've only a week. One week and then in rush the nasties. One week and school lets out. They'll flood my shop, just like every summer. Disrespectful little Philistines. Grubby little runts rubbing my lovely confections over their ugly little mugs. How low

have I sunk? I trained in Paris under the great Chuck Rutley! Now look at me. Living hand-to-mouth on the crumpled, damp dollars of children.

The trials continue. Both pumpkin chocolate-chip cookies and my own. How much longer can I last? How can I bear this burden?

The round one. Benny. Cursed Benny. He will not leave the shop.

June 3

Can't go on. I am suffocating under childish adoration.

School unleashed any day now. No progress on the P.C.C. cookies. If only I had the money to return to Paris. To open the patisserie I deserve. No, that the world deserves of me.

Filthy little animals. Children. Scummy gum-chewing sneaker-clad nose pickers. Germ-wallowing wet-willie bed wetters. Children! They mock me. They clamor for my pastries, my candies, my cakes. Then gobble them like garbage disposals chewing chicken scraps. A mockery! An obscene parody of the fine art of candy eating.

Big little Benny lingers still. Had to chase

him off with a broom at closing last night. Never seen any creature crave anything like that, not like Benny craves sugar. Nearly makes me puke. The way he stands in the window, drooling over the petits fours and napoleons. Disgusting, big little Benny.

One of those horrible Milkhammer twins had the nerve to pick its nose in my store. I threw a bucket of cold cake batter at them both.

"Charlie Argyle really hated kids," Chloe said, flipping ahead through the pages of the journal.

"So why did he make candy and pastries, then?" Milton asked, sitting behind a growing number of stacked bills.

"It's a mystery," said Chloe. "There was one kid named Benny that he really hated."

She flipped a few more pages ahead and kept reading.

June 4

The Milkhammer woman came, mother to those horrible twins. Lectured me for battering her children. I told her they needed sweetening. That was my little joke. She didn't laugh. I wonder if she even understood.

I gave her a box of cupcakes (dark-chocolate

cake with an orange-scented butter-cream icing.) Figured I could appease the cow. I should hate her. After all, she produced two such despicable little goblins. But could not help but be charmed—Mother Milkhammer ate the whole box right in front of the shop. No cupcakes for the twins.

I am drowning in despair! The P.C.C. cookies remain muffin caps at best. Baked pudding at worst. If there is a "Great Pumpkin," he's somewhere laughing at me.

Benny continues standing in my window, staring in at the pastries. I want to smash him.

Chloe skimmed over ten straight pages of slightly altered pumpkin chocolate-chip cookie recipes before arriving at the next entry.

June 8

Breakthrough! How could I have been so stupid? How could I have been so blind? The pumpkin is my demon. Thought I couldn't control the moisture. Forget canned pumpkin. Moving on. Making my own.

Could I condense pumpkin? A pumpkin paste? Can such things be? Perhaps even a pumpkin butter? Hope for the cookies springs anew. But cursed

fate! The children are released from school! The barbarians are coming.

"Holy mackerel," said Milton. Chloe looked up from the journal. Milton had a dozen stacks of twenty-dollar bills laid out before him, another bunch in his hand.

"There's twelve thousand, four hundred, and twenty dollars here," he said.

Chapter 9

Creepy and Nasty

"Let's steal all the money and burn this place down," said Milton.

"I'm not sure that's the right thing to do," said Chloe.

They eventually decided to take a hundred dollars, enough to get them back home. Their parents could mail Mr. Argyle a check for the borrowed money.

Despite Milton's better judgment, Chloe convinced him that they needed something more to eat than candy.

"Okay," said Milton reluctantly, "but only if real food involves peanut butter and bananas."

"Deal," said Chloe.

They decided to go into town and use part of their hundred dollars on groceries. At the supermarket on Main Street, they bought bread, peanut butter, bananas, chocolate milk, carrots, toothbrushes, and toothpaste.

When they got back to the Argyle house, they found Brad and Erica Milkhammer jumping rope on the street in front of the pumpkin patch. The Milkhammer twins were using an extralong rope, holding hands, and jumping together. They both noticed Milton and Chloe at the same time, and the rope became tangled in their feet.

"Are you the Nasselrogts?" asked half of the Milkhammer twins.

"I'm Milton," said the appropriate Nasselrogt, nodding, "and this is Chloe."

"Our names are Brad and Erica," said the other half of the Milkhammer twins.

"Nice to meet you," said Milton. Chloe's eyes darted from one twin to the other, trying to tell which one was Brad, and which was Erica. They looked exactly alike.

"Do you want to jump rope with us?" asked a Milkhammer.

Chloe shook her head.

"Chloe might," said Milton. "I have to take the groceries inside." He took the milk and bananas from Chloe and ran toward the house.

"You stand in the middle, we'll swing the rope," said half of the twins.

They stepped apart, and Chloe stepped nervously between them. The Milkhammers swung the rope and Chloe's feet were immediately tangled.

"Sorry," she said. "I'll try again."

The Milkhammers sighed, and swung the rope. Chloe jumped,

and again her feet were caught on the first swing.

"Come on," said half of the twins. "You're ruining the game."

"Sorry," Chloe said.

"We're trying to play with you," said the other half.

"Don't you want to play with us?"

"Yeah, yeah," said Chloe. "Can I try again?"

The Milkhammers shrugged at each other. Chloe got ready to jump, and then the rope swung beneath her and was instantly tangled in her feet. She suddenly realized what was happening.

One of the Milkhammer twins was swinging the rope in a dextrorotatory direction, the other was swinging the rope in a levorotatory direction. The two ends of the rope were swinging in opposite directions, crossing beneath Chloe. Even the world's greatest tap dancer (yours truly) could not have successfully skipped that rope.

"Why don't you jump the rope?" asked one of the Milkhammers.

"Don't you like us?" asked the other.

"Why won't you play with us?"

Chloe looked from one twin to the other.

"It's not my fault. . . ." she said.

"Oh, you think it's one of us?"

"Which one?"

Chloe was miserable.

"Maybe she thinks boys can't swing a jump rope," said one twin.

"Maybe that's it," said the other. They weren't even looking at Chloe, but at each other. All of the mirth missing from their mother's eyes gleamed in their own.

"No," said Chloe. If a rogue elephant were to come along and trample her at that moment, she would not have minded, just for the opportunity for escape.

"Chloe!" Milton shouted from the porch. "Come help me put the groceries away!"

Chloe could have showered Milton in gold (and would have thrown the first nugget extrahard for his having left her to the Milkhammers in the first place). She waved good-bye to the twins and ran toward the house.

"Hey," one of the twins said. Chloe looked back.

"Where's your uncle, Charlie Argyle?"

"I don't know," Chloe said, edging through the pumpkin patch.

"Do you know what happened in that house?" asked a twin.

Chloe stopped. "What happened?" she asked.

The twins shook their heads. Chloe couldn't tell whether they did not know, or they were too horrified to say.

"Your uncle's creepy," said a twin.

"A nasty man," said the other.

"A creepy and nasty man."

* * *

Milton made peanut-butter-and-banana sandwiches.

They wanted to eat dinner on the porch, but the Milkhammers were still outside, and the Nasselrogts would rather have gargled hornets than risk another conversation with the twins.

Milton and Chloe sat on the floor in the living room, eating sandwiches and carrots, taking turns drinking from the cardboard spout of the chocolate milk carton.

They brushed their teeth and went to bed early, so that they could wake at dawn to catch the bus home.

"It'll be good to see mom and dad," said Milton.

Chloe nodded, but did not say anything. She could imagine the orphans at Urchin House advising her about her parents: *They're either dead or they don't want you.*

"Back to the coal mines," Milton said to Beulah, as she opened the bus door.

"Good on ya," she said, and gave Chloe a wink. In return, Chloe gave her a peanut-butter-and-banana sandwich wrapped in wax paper, and a small box of Mr. Argyle's chocolates.

"Thanks for helping us the other day," said Chloe.

"Well, bless your heart," said Beulah.

It was a long ride with frequent stops in the dozens of tiny towns along their path. At every depot, Milton and Chloe looked out the window at families reuniting or parting, at children leaping from the bus and into the arms of their joyful parents.

They ate lunch with Beulah, who told them about her father. "Taught me everything he knew about mining," she said. "Broke his heart when I fell in love with a bus and with the road."

They chewed banana sandwiches.

"What are your parents like?" Beulah asked.

"They're good," said Milton.

"They work a lot," said Chloe.

"Everybody's gotta work," said Beulah. "That's the way of the world."

The sun had already clocked out, put on its hat, and was heading out the door by the time the bus reached the end of its route. Milton and Chloe shook Beulah's hand good-bye at the depot and caught a local bus back to their own neighborhood.

Chapter 10

The Nasselrogt Children Return Home and Everything Turns Out Fine

The sight of their home made Milton and Chloe go soft and sweet, like warm caramel. Milton enjoyed the occasional adventure, but he would not deny the relief of a homecoming.

The family station wagon was parked in the driveway, and the lights in the house were shining, casting over the lawn a warm glow that embraced the Nasselrogt children.

Neither noticed the khaki sedan parked across the street, out of lamplight's reach.

Chloe looked up at the waxing moon, bright and nearly full. *A full moon tomorrow night,* she thought.

"There they are!" Milton said, pointing at the dining room window.

Chloe looked up and caught a brief glimpse of her mom and dad passing through a doorway inside the house.

Milton broke into a run, Chloe right on his heels. He banged on the door.

"Mom! Dad! We're home!"

Too anxious to wait, he pulled the key chain from around his neck and unlocked the door, and the Nasselrogt children tumbled inside like bowled puppies.

"Mom! Dad!" they shouted, running toward the dining room.

"We're home!" They were grinning so hard that their faces hurt.

Milton's feet stomped across the kitchen. It was the only sound in the house.

"Mom!" he shouted once more. He turned and saw Chloe standing on the other side of the kitchen. She was looking off into the distance, listening.

Milton listened too. The house was absolutely silent.

"Mom? Dad? Where are you?"

They had seen their parents in the dining room only moments before. Now it was empty.

They don't want you. The orphan's words settled in Chloe's head and made themselves at home.

Had her mom and dad heard their children come home and hid? Tears shined in Chloe's eyes.

She turned away from Milton so that he would not see her cry. Her eyes lit on the framed Nasselrogt family portrait hanging near the stove. Her mom and dad smiled out of the picture at her, but Milton and Chloe's faces had been neatly cut out. There were only holes where their heads had been.

"We're home!" Milton shouted. He ran into the living room. It was empty. So, too, were the den, the back hallway, and every bedroom. He ran back into the kitchen, breathless.

Chloe was sitting on the floor.

"They were just here," said Milton. "You saw them too, right?"

Chloe nodded.

"I don't get it," said Milton.

"They don't want us."

"No . . ." Milton dug around for something to say and came up empty.

Chloe looked at the floor.

"Don't cry," said Milton.

"I'm not," said Chloe.

"If you cry, I'll leave you here," said Milton.

"I'm not crying!" she said, turning away from him.

Milton tried to think. The house was silent except for the faint humming of the air conditioner, unnecessary now that autumn had fallen. Maybe that was the reason for the chill.

Milton could hear his sister quoting the orphan: *They were either dead, or they don't want us.* They had seen their parents through the window, Milton was sure of that. They could not be dead. But then the only option . . .

A movement reflected in a dark window caught Milton's eye, and he turned.

"Mom!" he shouted.

Chloe looked up from the floor. All the hope and tenderness lost in the last few moments returned, spreading across her face in a grin that nearly creased her ears.

"Mom!" she cried. "Dad!"

The figure of their dad emerged slowly from the hall beyond the darkened doorway in which their mother stood. They could see him through their mother's face.

Milton took a step back.

"Mom?"

Their mother glided slowly forward, still partly obscured by darkness. She was completely transparent. Her mouth gaped open, and as she drifted toward them, it stretched impossibly wide, as if she were screaming but silent as death, a scream that had somehow gone beyond noise.

Chloe's scream was nowhere near so subtle.

Through the doorway, they saw their father lift off the ground and float into the air.

Chloe screamed again, her fists clutched at her sides.

Their mother's eyes were empty sockets, her hair gone. She was like a dim reflection in unwashed glass.

Milton retreated, shaking. He grabbed Chloe's hand and ran. They scrambled through the den and across the living room. Chloe knocked against a lamp, sending it shattering to the floor, the room thrown into shadow-cast gloom.

They hit the door to the garage, Milton yanked it open, and he and his sister swung through.

He hit the button for the garage door and it slowly, slowly began to rumble open. He dragged Chloe over to the door as it lifted off the cement floor one unbearable inch at a time.

"They're dead," said Chloe. "They're ghosts."

"There's no such thing as ghosts," Milton said, his legs shaking. The door rumbled slowly upward.

"They're ghosts," Chloe said again.

Milton pulled her to the ground and pushed her beneath the garage door ahead of him. He dropped onto his hands and knees, scuffling after her. . . .

The back of Milton's belt caught on the garage door handle.

"Unholy mackerel!" he shouted as he was pulled off the ground.

Chloe grabbed his hand and tugged, but with each tug, Milton's belt wrapped even tighter around the handle.

Suddenly, headlights burst out of the night, pinning the Nasselrogt children in their glare like spotlights in a prison break.

Chloe turned, Milton's hand still grasped in her own, and squinted into the light. She could not make out the dark figure that stepped from behind the driver's-side door.

"Help me!" Milton hissed, tugging on her arm. He was two feet off the ground by now. Chloe pulled again, succeeding only in drawing Milton's belt farther onto the handle.

"Hold it right there!" cried the voice behind the headlights.

Chloe knew that neat, clipped voice. She could see only the squat silhouette of a figure before the headlights' glare, but she recognized it as that of Mr. Porifera.

"You belong in Urchin House," Porifera said. "You belong *to* Urchin House."

Chloe turned back to Milton and pulled harder. He was four feet off the ground, legs kicking madly, as if pumping an imaginary bicycle. Chloe watched helplessly as the door slowly drew Milton upward.

Porifera's shadow fell over them, narrowing as he approached.

Chloe tugged on Milton's arm, her head snapping frantically between her brother's terrified eyes and Porifera's quickly approaching form.

Milton was high enough off the ground that Chloe was now pulling downward.

Both Nasselrogt children realized simultaneously what awaited Milton at the top of the garage door. When completely raised, the door sat flush against the ceiling. There was not nearly enough space between door and ceiling for an eleven-year-old boy. Milton would be crunched like toes caught in a hungry escalator.

Chloe pulled and pulled, but Milton was stuck fast.

Porifera's hand clamped onto Chloe's shoulder and wrenched her out of her brother's grasp.

Milton looked up and into the eyes of Mr. Porifera, into

those egg-yolky globes glimmering in triumph.

"Young Mr. Nasselrogt," he said, then looked down at Chloe. "How was my pronunciation?"

Chloe did not answer. Milton was being drawn steadily toward the crunch-point.

Porifera released Chloe's shoulder and reached up to her brother. He took Milton by the armpits and lifted him off of the garage door handle.

"You were trying to make a great deal of trouble for me, eh?" Porifera said, holding the boy before him. "Less trouble, more zippers from here on out, I think."

Milton looked at him and thought, *If only I had lobster claws.*

Porifera smiled. Finding the Nasselrogt children was like exhaling a breath he had been unable to release for days. He would keep his eye on them from now on. He would make sure they never escaped again.

The garage door finally reached the ceiling and rumbled to a stop. A sudden, somnolent suburban silence suffused the situation.

"Look," said Chloe.

Porifera's smile faltered. Milton saw his eyes dart toward the back of the garage, now revealed by the headlights of his sedan.

"What . . . ?" Porifera began, dropping Milton and taking a step backward.

The ephemeral figures of Mr. and Ms. Nasselrogt floated toward him.

Milton glanced back and saw them in the glare of the head-lights. They were like reflections in rippling water, tattered shreds of his mom and dad's images, floating above the ground.

Porifera was momentarily frozen; he had no place to file this experience. He would not believe in ghosts.

Milton sprang like a mousetrap, grabbing Chloe's hand and sprinting away into the night.

Chapter 11

The Last Chapter Title Was Obviously a Big Lie

My sincerest apologies.[4]

4 Another fabrication.

Chapter 12

Dove in the Pants

The Nasselrogt children, frightened and confused, ran back the way they had come.

Porifera's khaki sedan was waiting for them outside the bus depot. So Milton stumbled frantically on, dragging Chloe toward the last place they had seen their parents alive. They flung themselves through the revolving doors and into the shopping mall, twenty minutes before closing time.

The security guard did not see them sprint into the department store, past the tanning booths, and on toward the trouser racks that stood guard between the Home Spa and Hefty Boy sections.

They dove in the pants rack where their troubles had started so seemingly long ago. Crouching, knees touching, they tried to catch their breath.

"We can sleep here tonight," Milton said.

"They're ghosts—they're dead," said Chloe.

Milton looked at her. Chloe was looking at the ground.

"We can't stay in town," Milton said. "Porifera's here. We *can't* go back to Urchin House." He wearily eyed the dozens of zippers circled around them, now a dour reminder of the orphanage.

"Mom and Dad are dead," Chloe said again, softly.

"I . . . I don't want to talk about it," Milton said. "We need to figure out what we're going to do."

Chloe did not respond.

"If we go to anybody we know, Porifera will find us."

Chloe looked at the ground.

"Luckily, we don't know anybody," said Milton.

"How could they have died?" Chloe asked. "We were only in here for a few seconds."

"Shut up!" Milton hissed. "We can't worry about that now. We have to . . ."

Chloe continued to stare at the ground, dry-eyed.

"Be tough," Milton commanded.

The department store loudspeaker announced that the mall would be closing in five minutes.

"I think we should go back to Goodfellow's Landing. We can stay in the Argyle house until we figure things out," Milton said.

Chloe nodded. She pulled an XXXL pair of pants from the rack, wrapped herself in corduroy, and waited for the lights to go out so that she could cry without her brother seeing.

But there is no such thing as dusk in a shopping mall. As the fluorescent lights flickered throughout the night, Chloe's tears, eager to wash her face, welled up inside of her, but she would not let them out. Eventually, she fell asleep. Her eyes were dry, but she was filled to the brim with sorrow.

The next morning, Porifera's sedan was waiting in front of the bus depot like a khaki tiger ready to pounce. The Nasselrogt children crawled on their bellies past the driver's-side door, and slipped inside the depot undetected.

Milton and Chloe used the last of Charlie Argyle's hundred dollars to buy breakfast and bus tickets back to Goodfellow's Landing.

The bus driver was not Beulah, which was just as well; neither of the Nasselrogts felt rambunctious enough to fib.

As the bus pulled away from the depot, Chloe gazed dolefully through the window, not really seeing anything. She thought about never seeing her parents again, or her hometown, or any of the things that had been her childhood.

Good-bye to little Chloe, she thought, and gave a small wave to her reflection in the glass.

Porifera woke in his car with a stiff neck and lingering memories of a dream about a zipper with hundreds of tiny Nasselrogt children where the teeth should have been.

In the depot, he used the pay phone to check on Urchin House. It was still there, getting by without him. Zipper production marched on.

Then he called the hospital, to check on Mr. and Ms. Nasselrogt.

"They have another day of moisturization," said the nurse on the other end of the phone, "and then they'll be heading back home."

Porifera rubbed his eyes. That meant he had only one day to find Chloe and Milton. He shook his head, thinking of last night's "ghost" scare and what had *really* happened to their parents.

Sunburned skin *peels*.

In the case of the world's worst tan, Mr. and Ms. Nasselrogt's leathered skin had sloughed off like a snake's, paper-thin shells of their entire forms slipping off and floating raggedly in the currents of the air-conditioned house.

The shedding had left Mr. and Ms. Nasselrogt as soft and pink as newborn mice, inspiring a three-day trip to the hospital to be rubbed with calamine lotion and fed Jell-O.

Porifera had waited outside the Nasselrogt house for a night and a day before Milton and Chloe showed up, then blown his one chance to apprehend them with his silly fear that the shed skins were ghosts. Porifera filed himself under "Foolish."

Walking back to his car, he was nearly run over by an outbound bus. He stumbled back in surprise, a surprise quickly doubled by the sight of Chloe Nasselrogt gazing out of the window, almost directly at Porifera, and waving good-bye.

Porifera filed himself under "Determined" and ran back into the depot.

The man behind the ticket counter gave him the names of the

seventeen towns in which that particular bus was scheduled to stop. Porifera was back on the trail.

Goodfellow's Landing was now oddly familiar to the Nasselrogt children. Walking through the sleepy streets toward the Argyle house felt like a kind of homecoming.

Chloe almost sloshed with despair, so many tears had built up inside of her. She was determined not to cry in front of her brother, and marched along beside him with her mouth clamped shut.

Milton was exhausted, having slept little the night before and not at all on the bus. He was scheming madly, overwhelmed by the sudden responsibility of taking care of himself, never mind the burden of caring for Chloe.

We could join the circus, he thought. *I'll swallow chainsaws and juggle fire, and Chloe can sweep the elephant cage.* But Milton realized he would never make it in show business with his chubby ankles.

We could become bank robbers, was another idea. *Nobody would suspect children.* But Milton knew he couldn't wear panty hose over his face without giggling, and nobody would respect a giggling bank robber.

We'll become astronauts, he thought. *Porifera will never find us on the moon!* But Chloe's claustrophobia would never allow her to get into a rocket, much less a space suit. He eyed Chloe. She could be so troublesome.

All seemed hopeless to poor Milton.

The pumpkin patch had grown noticeably in their two-day absence. The little dark-green buds were now the size of golf balls and webbed with intricate veins. The vines had thickened and curled, climbing over one another, and were more difficult to navigate.

The bananas were all gone, so they ate peanut-butter-and-nothing sandwiches for dinner.

Milton insisted on leaving a nightlight on as they slept. Chloe, needing desperately to cry, would have preferred darkness.

"I'm going outside for a second," she said.

"What for?" asked Milton.

"To check on the pumpkin patch."

"Okay." Milton lay down on the couch as Chloe walked out the door.

The pumpkin patch! he thought, wondering how he had missed seeing the opportunity before. They would become farmers. Halloween was not far away; everybody in Goodfellow's Landing would need a pumpkin.

"The Nasselrogt Patch," Milton whispered aloud.

As soon as she stepped off of the porch, the tears began to stream down Chloe's face. She picked her way through the vines, tears falling like raindrops onto the thirsty soil beneath the newborn pumpkins.

She circled through the patch, around the house, and up the hill.

Unlike Milton, she could not distract herself from thoughts of her parents' ghosts by scheming about the future. Every time she closed her eyes, she saw their tattered, ghostly forms.

She remembered her mother singing "My Melancholy Baby" to her, her earliest memory:

Come to me, my melancholy baby.
Cuddle up and don't be blue.
All your fears are foolish fancies, maybe . . .

She tripped over a vine, now crying freely, tears shining on her cheeks in the light of the full moon.

Halfway up the hill, she sat down on a bare patch of dirt and let the rest of the tears flood out.

Chloe's crying was epic and exhausting. If Noah had seen it, he might have begun construction of an ark.

Milton, behind the living room window, could do nothing but watch.

Chloe did not notice the soil shifting and trembling underneath the pumpkin patch. Thirsty vines drank their fill of her tears.

Chapter 13

Pink Banana Jumbo, Dickinson Munchkin

By the time Chloe had woken the next morning, Milton had been up for hours, candy-powered, composing his Plan of Action.

The first page of the plan read:

1. GROW PUMPKINS
2. SELL PUMPKINS

The next page was a list of subobjectives:

—learn to grow pumpkins
—paint a sign
—buy a suit

"What's the suit for?" Chloe asked, rubbing the sleep from her eyes.

"To sell pumpkins in," said Milton.

"We need clothes," said Chloe. "I've been wearing the same socks for five days."

"We're broke until step two," said Milton, putting a finger on SELL PUMPKINS. "Unless . . ."

Milton put his pencil to page two and added:

—steal Charlie Argyle's money

"Problem solved!" he said to Chloe. She did not smile, so in hopes of cheering her up he added to the list:

—buy Chloe socks

"Thanks," said Chloe. "We'll also need to buy real food, and we'll need to clean up the house."

Neither grocery shopping nor housekeeping appealed greatly to Milton, but Chloe's tears of the night before had frightened him.

"Sure, sure," he said, adding her chores to the list as Chloe made herself toast for breakfast.

They quickly accomplished their "steal Charlie Argyle's money" chore, then walked into town to buy groceries and clothes.

Clothing was purchased without incident. At the department store they each bought a week's worth of pants, shirts, undies, and socks. At the thrift shop nearby, Milton bought a three-piece suit, pinstriped and complete with vest and hula-girl tie. September's gray chill was descending on Goodfellow's Landing, so Milton bought a carrot-orange scarf and Chloe bought a red hooded sweat-shirt with a kangaroo pouch in the front.

"Why aren't you kids in school?" asked the man at the register.

"We're new in town," said Milton.

"Where *is* the school?" asked Chloe.

"Underneath the water tower." The cashier hooked his thumb over his shoulder.

"We'll go get enrolled," said Chloe.

Milton wished he had been drinking something so that he could have sprayed it from his mouth in shock.

Milton convinced Chloe to hold off on school until the follow-ing day, and they spent the rest of the afternoon in the Argyle house.

Chloe took up Argyle's "Pumpkin/Chocolate Trials" and began reading where she had left off.

"Paint a sign" was the next activity on Milton's list, so he set about finding a board and some paint. Ten minutes of searching revealed no such arts and crafts materials.

"Did you look in the basement?" Chloe asked.

He had not. She pointed out the door and went back to her reading.

The basement was as dark as a well, even in the middle of the day. From the top of the stairs Milton could only barely see rows of gleaming crescents in the darkness.

He descended the stairs into the gloom, firmly gripping the banister.

"There's something down here," he called back to Chloe, who was engrossed in Argyle's journal.

As he reached the packed-dirt floor, the dim light from the top of the stairs began to fade. Milton realized that the door was slowly swinging itself shut.

Milton cast frantically about in the quickly dimming light. There was a string dangling in the center of the basement and he yanked on it, illuminating a single bare bulb moments before the closing door cast him entirely into darkness.

The crescent reflections were jars. Milton was surrounded by them, his own warped reflection staring back from hundreds of dusty glass cylinders filled with dark-brown goop. The jars were labeled with handwritten strips of masking tape.

Milton squinted at the labels. One read BOSTON MARROW / BROWN SUGAR / 4 HOURS; another read DICKINSON MUNCHKIN / MOLASSES / 3 HOURS. Yet another read GHOST RIDER / BROWN SUGAR / 6 HOURS. The goop in the jars looked like chocolate applesauce.

On the far side of the basement there were smaller jars, each filled with a different variety of what Milton recognized as pumpkin seeds. They, too, were labeled: HOWDEN. PINK BANANA JUMBO. DICKINSON MUNCHKIN. DICKINSON MAMMOTH. JACK-BE-LITTLE. GHOST RIDER.

"Ah," said Milton. *The goop in the larger jars must be made from pumpkin.*

A jar caught his eye. It was nestled among the seed jars but filled with something green, white, and silver—something shredded, like coleslaw mixed with nails.

Milton held the jar up to the light. It was filled with torn-up cash and a few silver dollars.

"Weird," observed Milton. He shook the jar of cash coleslaw. It *shushed* like footsteps in grass, the few coins clinking pleasantly against the glass.

A workbench covered in tools waited in the corner of the basement. Among various confectioner's gadgets and farming tools Milton found three cans of paint and a brush with bristles stiff as a mustache.

Now all he needed was something to serve as the sign itself. There was an old coffee table leaning against the wall with all but one of its legs missing.

"That'll do," he said, grabbing the remaining leg and pulling on it until it popped off like the stem of a rotten pumpkin.

"Chloe!" she heard her brother's voice, muffled, calling her from beyond the basement door. She marked her place and put down the "Pumpkin/Chocolate Trials." When she opened the basement door, she found Milton standing on the top step with the doorknob in his hand.

"It came off in my hand," he said, pushing the knob back onto its spindle. "We'll have to fix that."

The thought almost depressed Chloe; the idea of making repairs to the house seemed to suggest that they would be staying for a long time.

As she returned to the sofa and curled up with Charlie Argyle's journal, Milton noisily dragged the amputee coffee table up the stairs, along with three jars of the brown goop.

"The basement's filled with some kind of pumpkin stuff," Milton said, showing her a jar labeled DICKINSON MAMMOTH / BROWN SUGAR / 5 HOURS.

"It's pumpkin butter," said Chloe. "You eat it on toast."

"How do you know?" asked Milton.

"In here." She held up Argyle's journal.

Milton laid what was left of the coffee table on the floor. He had white, black, and red paint. He started by painting the whole table red so it would act like a stop sign, making people pause and peruse the pumpkins. He then painted THE NASSELROGT PATCH in eight-inch-tall black letters. He was halfway through outlining the letters in white when Chloe interrupted him.

"That man is still watching us," she said.

"Who?" Milton looked up from his sign.

"In the house across the street."

Milton stood and looked out the window. Indeed, the dark figure of a man was still visible in the front window of the avocado-green house.

"Creepy," said Milton.

Chloe nodded.

Their view was suddenly obscured, as a big yellow school bus, squealing like a cannon-shot piglet, pulled to a stop in front of the house. The doors opened and the Milkhammer twins descended to the street.

Instinctively, both Milton and Chloe drew away from the window.

"Oh, great," said Milton. "If we go to school tomorrow, we get to hang out with the Milkhammers."

Chloe did not take the bait. She let her gaze fall back down onto the "Pumpkin/Chocolate Trials" as Milton returned to his sign.

"All we have left after this," said Milton, "is learning how to grow pumpkins and then waiting to sell them."

"I know how to grow pumpkins," said Chloe, holding up Argyle's journal. "It's in here."

"Terrific," said Milton. "Anything else interesting in there?"

There was.

Chapter 14

The Pumpkin/Chocolate Trials, June 9–20

Along with the ever-evolving pumpkin chocolate-chip cookie recipes filling the pages of the journal, Chloe began to find drawings of various breeds of pumpkin, sketches detailing canning techniques, and mailing addresses for seed- and farm-supply companies.

Scattered in between all that, a little more than a week's worth of history:

> *June 9*
> The children are set loose. Somebody needs to put a bounty on the filthy little apes. I have no peace. Can't practice my craft. No time to experiment.
>
> Work replaces sleep. In the dark hours I can *work*.
>
> Pumpkin butter! A revelation! A giant leap in the P.C.C. cookies. Almost achieved a crisp cookie!

(Note to self—separate journal for pumpkin spice gingersnaps.) I'm getting close.

Factory-made pumpkin butter is jarred poop. Fit for invalids and children. Babies without teeth. I make my own:

PUMPKIN BUTTER, 6.9

BAKE AT 350⁰ UNTIL VERY SOFT

10 lbs. pumpkin

PUREE WITH
1 C. honey
4 t. cinnamon
2 t. cloves
2 t. ginger
1/2 t. nutmeg
1/2 t. mace
1/4 t. white pepper
1 t. salt
3-5 T. cider vinegar
2-3 C. dark-brown sugar

COOK ON A STOVETOP OVER MEDIUM HEAT, STIRRING CONSTANTLY UNTIL

THICK, ABOUT HALF AN HOUR.

Cook that stovetop for half an hour, you've got spread for toast. Spread that on a baking sheet and cook for two hours, you've got <u>pumpkin</u> <u>paste</u>. Now you're making cookies.

June 13
    Chelsey, Ghost Rider, Rouge Vif d'Estampes, Buckskin, Dickinsons, Green-Striped Cushaw, Triple Treat, Munchkin. Pumpkins, pumpkins, pumpkins. So far the Buckskin bakes down the best. Sweetest taste, the most complex.
    Finding pumpkins in midsummer: not easy. I'm writing letters. I'm making phone calls. I've got a contact in Vermont, he knows some guys in Canada. I'm having pumpkins smuggled across the border. I'm realizing there's a <u>Winter Squash Underground</u>. I'm picking up hints. There are types of pumpkin the public doesn't know about.
    I hate children.

Several pages contained a sketched map of Argyle's yard, with different areas of the pumpkin patch labeled for different breeds. On the next page, scrawled in angry letters:

June 14

I am a furnace of rage. I had been cooking down a Rouge Vif d'Estampes pumpkin, which had cost me a day's salary. Was distracted by a noise in the back. Found Benny going through my Dumpster. The Dumpster's where he belongs.

The brat's been stealing my garbage! Eating my discarded P.C.C. cookie experiments! I'm throwing out dozens of dozens daily, who knows how many he's been eating. Benny had the nerve to tell me they were good. My failures! <u>Good</u>! I could smash him.

I've kicked him out of the shop. Persona non grata. He's lost his pastry privileges. I put a sign in the window, BENNY NOT WELCOME.

Returned to the kitchen to find my Rouge Vif d'Estampes burned. A night's experiments wasted. Cursed Benny!

"Charlie Argyle took away Benny's pastry privileges—kicked him out of the store," said Chloe.

"What for?" asked Milton.

"He was stealing pumpkin chocolate-chip cookies from the bakery's garbage."

"Those cookies are starting to sound good," said Milton. Chloe skimmed through the journal, past shopping lists and more crude cartoons of Benny on fire, before finding the next entry.

> *June 17*
> Pumpkin, the Buckskin variety, using buck-wheat honey, light-brown sugar, oven-cooked for five hours. Best results so far. I have my pumpkin butter.
> Interesting news from the Squash Under-ground. There is a pumpkin/squash hybrid. Squampkins. If it could capture the sweetness of butternut, with the complexity of pumpkin . . . Hard to get my hands on squampkins. My sup-plier seems almost afraid of them . . .
> Benny's father came into the shop today. Tall man, thin. He begged me to let his son back in the shop. Said his boy cries himself to sleep at nights if he doesn't have some puff pastry. I sent Benny's dad packing.

"Squampkins?" asked Milton, "like the box."

"That's what it says," said Chloe, not lifting her eyes from the pages.

June 19

Benny watches the shop from across the street. He wants pastries bad. He can get them somewhere else. I'm keeping my garbage indoors.

I can't be sure the dozens of other horrible little apes aren't buying sweets for him. But Benny seems like a loner. I don't think he has friends.

I'm close on the P.C.C. cookies. Adjusting fat ratios, oven temperatures. Should have perfection in a matter of days.

June 20

Squampkin seeds. Interesting. My contact says you can only get squampkins by growing them yourself.

The seeds came in a box locked down on four sides. Makes the seeds seem dangerous. I rattle the box and the seeds rattle back.

There's bad mojo in squampkins. Nobody wants to say exactly what.

Chapter 15

Figure in the Squampkin Patch

The pumpkin-growing instructions were torn from a magazine featuring a photo of a coverall-clad farmer standing next to an enormous pumpkin of which he seemed in equal parts proud and frightened.

Chloe handed the page to Milton and continued to study the journal.

"We might have squampkins in our field," she said.

Our field, thought Milton, with no small pride, looking down at the large red "Nasselrogt Patch" sign so near completion.

"What's a squampkin?" he asked.

"Half pumpkin and half squash. And maybe a little dangerous," said Chloe.

"Dangerous how?"

Chloe shook her head rather than answer, and walked into the kitchen to chip some sugar off of the boulder to read by. The electric lights in the living room worked, but Chloe had grown fond of reading by the toffee-scented glow of a sugar flame.

Milton's eyes scanned the magazine page. If baby pumpkins

were already showing on the vine, all they had to do was see that the field was watered.

"Great," said Milton. "The pumpkins take care of themselves."

"Squampkins," corrected Chloe, returning with a sugar chip on a saucer and a box of matches.

"Right," Milton said, satisfied that the closest thing to farming they would have to do was rake in the cash. He looked out the window. Autumn evening had settled on the world outside. A breeze seemed to stir the squampkin patch; small twigs and runners quivered in the waxing moon.

"Dangerous how?" Milton asked again.

"I'm still reading," Chloe said.

Across the street, Milton could still see the man in the avocado house standing silhouetted in his window. No breeze moved the trees in his yard.

They shared a pumpkin-butter dinner. The "Five-Hour Buckskin Pumpkin Butter" was too thick to be enjoyed, it nearly had to be chewed separate from the toast. Milton opened seven jars, deciding that the "Half-Hour Ghostrider" was the best by far.

They brushed their teeth, spread their blankets in the living room, and went to bed.

Chloe woke hours before dawn, peed, and drank a glass of water (walking to the appropriate room before each step in the operation).

* * *

As she was lowering herself back into her nest of blankets, she glanced outside and noticed that the front window of the avocado house was finally empty. Maybe the watcher had gone to bed.

But there was a figure in the squampkin patch.

Chloe stopped breathing.

It was the same man, tall, thin. In profile, his nose was unnaturally large and sharp, like some obscure gardening tool. He was stepping carefully between the vines, still no more than a dark silhouette against the yellowish sodium glow of the streetlights.

A gust of wind picked leaves off the enormous tree on top of the hill and sent them fluttering through the air around him. As he turned into the wind, Chloe caught a first glimpse of something long in his hand, maybe a cane.

"Milton," Chloe whispered.

The man in the squampkin patch picked his way slowly through the vines, moving toward the house.

"Milton," Chloe hissed, louder.

The moonlight glinted for a moment off the metal head of whatever object the man was carrying. He was coming closer.

"Milton," Chloe said, kicking the sofa.

Milton was having that marshmallow-avalanche dream. He was halfway through eating his way out, and preferred not to be woken.

The man paused in the squampkin patch, looking down.

Chloe kicked her brother in the head.

"Walnuts," he said, eyes still closed.

Chloe kicked him in the head again.

Milton woke, groaned, and sat up.

Behind him, through the bay window, Chloe saw the man in the squampkin patch reach down and handle one of the baby gourds clinging to the gnarled vines. His teeth flashed momentarily in the darkness, a moonlit grimace.

"These aren't marshmallows at all," said Milton, disappointedly pulling the blankets off of his chest.

"There's somebody in the squampkin patch," said Chloe.

Milton turned to the window, his elbow knocking against a pane of glass.

At the sound, the man's gaze darted up toward the house. He sprang into motion, still in a crouch, running low and fast across the squampkin patch and into the darkness.

Milton rubbed his eyes.

Chloe watched the man vanish. Dead leaves tumbled through the air, flitting across the patch.

"Where?" asked Milton.

"He's gone," said Chloe. "It was the man from the avocado house. He was in our patch."

Neither of the Nasselrogt children slept through the remainder of the night.

Since Milton's sleep consisted mainly of marshmallow dreams, he reasoned that marshmallow reality would make a fine substitute. He opened another box of Charlie Argyle's candy and munched as he finished outlining the letters on the "Nasselrogt Patch" sign.

Chloe spent the night flipping through Argyle's recipe books and journal, searching for information on squampkins.

Near dawn, she found a creased business card stuck by a magnet to the refrigerator. The front of the card had GARDNER GRAY written across it in greasy pencil. Chloe flipped the card over. On the back, in handwriting that looked as much like a swarm of hungry ants as letters, was written this sentence:

"What you sow, they will reap."

Chapter 16

An Unexpected Gob

A person could have described the sky as orange or blue and been right in either case. It looked almost like sugar on fire. Dawn was teetering on the edge but had not yet broken when Milton dragged the legless coffee table he had painted into a "Nasselrogt Patch" sign up the hill. He had a hammer hanging from his belt and a pocket full of nails.

A corner of the sign dragged through the squampkin patch, carving a shallow trench in the soil and scraping roughly over the exposed vines. The vines twisted with the pressure and drew away from the earth, lifting squampkins now the size of baseballs. A little orange, the same shade as Milton's scarf, showed in the small gourds, under a thick spiderwebbing of dark-green veins.

Milton was winded by the time he reached the bare patch of earth beneath the great box elder at the top of the hill. He stood catching his breath, hands on hips, and looked up at the regal sentinel of a tree.

It was thick, gray, and twisted, like an elephant that had been wrung out to dry. Its lowest limbs were thirty feet off the ground at least, twisted branches that snaked off in all directions, several reaching well over the Argyle house.

Milton propped his "Nasselrogt Patch" masterpiece against the tree with his knee, and used the hammer to bend nails in against the sign until it gave up and held onto the tree so that the boy would stop abusing it.

The hilltop was one of the first places to catch the morning sun. Peach-colored light poured over the great box elder, making it glow like the skin of your hand when you shine a flashlight through it.

Milton loved this. The pride of ownership warmed his belly. *The Nasselrogt Patch.*

He was standing in the street grinning at his own work when Chloe emerged from the house with her red hooded sweatshirt and two brown paper bags.

As she picked her way through the squampkin patch, Milton said, "Look at that."

He nodded his head toward the sign. Chloe looked back, smiled in appreciation, and then toppled over, her ankle snagged in a vine.

Milton giggled.

Chloe pushed herself up onto her hands and knees, and found she was looking down at the impression of a large boot. She lifted her head and saw others leading away between the vines.

"Boot prints," she said.

Milton looked at the prints. They were evidence that last night's intruder had been more than his sister's strange dream.

Chloe continued to stare at the ground.

"Do you hear that?" she asked.

"Hear what?" Milton was still looking at the boot prints.

Chloe lowered her head and put an ear to the slightly damp, black soil. There was a faint gurgling sound deep in the earth.

"It sounds like . . ." she could not name the sound. It was like some deep reptilian breathing. Or a slowly bubbling stew. Or . . .

The squampkin patch was purring at her.

Sunlight crested the houses behind them and fell across the patch. The underground gurgling stopped.

Chloe got to her feet and shook the dirt from her ear.

"Sounds like what?" Milton asked.

Chloe shook her head and looked up at the rising sun.

"We're going to be late for school," she said. Milton sighed.

"There's nobody telling us we have to go to school," he said.

Chloe stooped among the vines and retrieved the two brown paper bags. She held one up.

"I packed you a lunch," she said.

Milton trudged behind Chloe toward the water tower, looking up every once and again to check for fire trucks or asteroids heading for their intended destination. No such luck.

The school waited for them like a squat brick toad waiting for sneaker-clad flies. Empty school buses lined the front drive, freshly unburdened of their mobs of children.

Chloe picked up her pace. Milton looked around frantically, certain that there was an impending earthquake or an army of Huns *somewhere* close enough to be useful.

Even worse: a khaki sedan parked by the entrance.

"Holy mackerel," said Milton.

Chloe was walking right past it.

Milton dashed to his sister and shoved her into some shrubbery.

"Milton!" Chloe said, scrambling in the tangle of branches. "What are you *umph*!" she said as Milton leaped into the bushes after her.

The front door of the school opened and a woman whose haircut screamed *Principal*! walked out next to Y. K. K. Porifera.

The Nasselrogts lay as still as stones pretending they were very frightened children.

Porifera was saying, ". . . I only want to bring them back to the care of Urchin House before they bring themselves harm."

"Of course." The principal said. She shifted a roll of posters to her other arm to shake Porifera's hand.

"And I do hope that if you find them"—Porifera refused to release the principal's hand as the words slithered like eels over his lips—"you'll call me before the police. Fugitive children can panic before authority."

"Completely understood," the principal said, withdrawing her hand as if it had just discovered an unexpected gob of pudding in her purse. She walked back into the school without saying good-bye.

On his way back to his car, Porifera stopped to tape a poster to a utility pole.

Even from their hideout in the shrubs, Milton and Chloe recognized their photographs on the poster, clipped from the family portrait in the Nasselrogt kitchen.

They waited until Porifera had climbed back into his sedan and driven out of sight before they burst from the shrubs, ripped the poster from the pole, and ran for the Argyle house.

A safe distance from the school, they read the words on the poster.

FUGITIVE CHILDREN!
Chloe Nasselrogt, Age 8, & Milton Nasselrogt,
Age 11
Caution, Milton and Chloe are FUGITIVE
ORPHANS, and potentially DANGEROUS. If
discovered, contact immediately:
MR. YON KINSKY KOZINSKY PORIFERA
URCHIN HOUSE
(a home for wayward children*)

Below that, a phone number and address were listed. And below that:

*** Mr. Porifera may also be contacted for all
zipper sales inquiries.**

"I'd like to explain how I feel about this," said Milton, rolling up the poster, "but we're not allowed to use those words."

"Me too," said Chloe. "We can't go to school, can we?" she kicked at a pebble on the road, frustrated and sad.

Good old Chloe, thought Milton. *Always there to find the silver lining.*

They walked quickly home, keeping a wary eye out for Porifera's car.

They found instead more FUGITIVE CHILDREN posters.

By the time they reached the Argyle house, they had ripped down and rolled up nearly two dozen of them.

Porifera used the pay phone on the edge of town to check in at Urchin House. No one had telephoned in a response to the FUGITIVE CHILDREN posters he had taped up in the first twelve towns along the route of the bus the Nasselrogt children had taken. Four more towns, and he would have covered every possible avenue of escape.

"What about their parents? Are they still telephoning?" Porifera asked. Mr. and Ms. Nasselrogt had been calling Urchin House hourly since they had returned from the hospital days earlier.

"No," said Porifera's assistant. "They've stopped calling altogether."

"Hmm," Porifera said. This was a curious thing.

"There will be more of those posters at school," Milton said.

"I think we should leave town," Chloe said.

"Where would we go?" Milton asked.

Chloe very nearly said *Home*, but the thought of her parents' ghosts silenced her.

"We have a house and money if we stay here," Milton said, adding, "and candy."

Chloe nodded.

"And I want to sell pumpkins," Milton said.

"They're squampkins."

"Squampkins."

"What do we do if Mr. Argyle comes back?" Chloe asked.

"We'll burn that bridge when we get to it," Milton answered. "This afternoon, after school lets out, I'll go back and tear down the rest of the posters."

Chloe nodded, thinking. The Nasselrogt children had lived pretty simple lives until they had ducked into the trouser rack. Now there was such an awful lot for Chloe to keep her mind on.

* * *

That afternoon, Milton watered the squampkin patch, the thirsty vines sucking greedily at the dampened soil.

Margery Milkhammer, jogging past, must have been surprised to see him. She stared at him so fixedly that she jogged into a mailbox, breaking it off of its post.

Milton considered turning the hose on her to make sure she was okay, but decided to ask instead.

"I'm fine," she said. "Poor Mr. Helsabeck's mailbox broke my fall."

"Mr. Helsabeck?" Milton asked. Where did he know that name? From the "Pumpkin/Chocolate Trials": *Helsabeck! He got to the patch before me!*

"Do you think he saw?" Milkhammer asked, trying to push the box back down onto the post.

"No," Milton said, looking at the avocado house. For once, Mr. Helsabeck was not staring out of the bay window. "What's wrong with Mr. Helsabeck?"

"Why should something be wrong with him?" Milkhammer narrowed her eyes at Milton, hungry for gossip.

"You said 'poor Mr. Helsabeck.'"

"No, no, no. When I said 'poor,' I meant his mailbox," Milkhammer said. "But James is 'poor' too."

"James . . ." Milton was trying to keep up.

"James Helsabeck. Lots of tragedy in that man's life. And now his mailbox . . ." She gave up trying to reattach the box to the post. "Here, hold this while I get some tools."

She shoved the box into Milton's hands and jogged back the way she had come.

Milton stood holding the mailbox and puzzling over tragic Mr. Helsabeck for several minutes. Margery Milkhammer did not appear to be coming back anytime soon.

In the avocado house, the living room curtains parted, and the silhouette of James Helsabeck stepped up to the glass.

As Milton watched Helsabeck, he felt that uncomfortably warm sensation that accompanies the gaze of a stranger, a sensation similar to swimming beside that kid with poor bladder control. He was being watched in return.

Milton put down the mailbox, turned around, and ran into Charlie Argyle's house. He convinced Chloe to go outside and turn off the hose.

Halloween decorations were materializing all over town. In the window of the hardware store, a mechanical green witch tilted her head back again and again, shaking with laughter. Cardboard jack-o'-lanterns were pasted in the supermarket windows between the specials.

Walking to the school, Milton waved to the woman at the thrift store, who was posing a Frankenstein's monster with movable joints. The thrift store woman used the monster's green cardboard hand to wave back.

Milton loved an empty school. He could not resist sprinting down the abandoned hallways, just to hear his sneakers slap against the tiles.

There were no FUGITIVE CHILDREN! posters. On several walls, Milton found four ripped corners taped up, as if a poster had been torn down from the middle. But the signs themselves were gone.

This should have been some small relief to Milton. But, instead, it somehow gave him that somebody-peed-in-the-pool sensation.

The Milkhammer twins stood on the street-side edge of the squampkin patch, squinting up at Milton's sign.

Chloe watched them talking from the front window of the Argyle house, hoping Milton would come home so she would not have to talk to the two.

But when Brad and Erica Milkhammer started across the squampkin patch and up the hill to the box elder, Chloe reluctantly left the house.

The Milkhammers were studying the sign up close, standing beneath the great twisted tree as an autumn wind chased the last of the day's light southward.

Chloe realized she had an opportunity to finally differentiate the two.

"Brad!" she called out as she climbed the hill.

Neither of the twins turned their attention from the sign.

"Erica!" she tried.

The twins turned like interconnected cogs, simultaneously rotating to face her.

"Yes?" one said.

"Yes?" said the other.

"Oh, which one of us were you talking to?"

Chloe wished she had a hole she could crawl into. Or a larger hole she could push the twins into.

"What are you guys doing?" she asked.

"We like your sign," said a twin.

"Yes, very much so," said the other. "Because we saw this word earlier today." The twin pointed at NASSELROGT, writ large by Milton's hand.

"But when we saw it earlier, we thought there might have been some mistake," said one twin.

"Because our mom said that your name was Nasal Rod," said the other.

"And even though the pictures on the posters looked like you . . ."

". . . and even though the children's first names were Milton and Chloe . . ."

". . . their last name was Nazz Ell Wroghtee."

"So we took the posters down so you wouldn't get into trouble."

One twin reached for the other's backpack and unzipped it, revealing a crumpled mass of FUGITIVE CHILDREN! posters. The twin rezipped the backpack, the sound of the zipper crawling up Chloe's spine like red ants.

"What do you want?" Chloe asked.

The Milkhammer twins let their mischievous eyes meet momentarily.

"Is this how you spell Nasal Rod?" one of them asked, pointing at Milton's sign.

Chloe nodded.

"What does 'fugitive' mean?" asked the other.

"Runaway," said Chloe. It wasn't just an answer; it was what she wanted to do.

Both twins shook their heads.

"We checked the dictionary . . ."

". . . which said 'fugitive' means 'criminal.'"

They waited for Chloe to speak. When she did not, one Milkhammer turned to the other as if suddenly struck by a great thought.

"You know," said the twin, "sometimes there's a reward for information leading to the capture of a criminal."

"You know, I've heard the same thing," said the other.

"Though there's nothing on the poster about a reward."

"Well, it couldn't hurt to call and check."

"To call Mr. Porifera and check for a reward?"

"It couldn't hurt."

"Well . . . it couldn't hurt *us*." The Milkhammers let their eyes slowly sweep back over to Chloe. They grinned like cats who had cornered a mouse on crutches.

Chapter 17

Cruelty for the Macaroons

Milton heard the banging several blocks from the Argyle house. He quickened his pace. Streetlights were slowly blinking to life in the gloaming.

"Hi, Milton," said a nearby voice, clogged with caramel.

Milton looked over and saw the Milkhammer twins sitting on their front steps, each eating a box of Charlie Argyle's candy.

Milton was agog. In fact, he was two gogs and one and a half ghasts. The Milkhammer twins grinned with chocolate-smeared teeth and waved.

The banging was coming from the Argyle house. Milton walked even faster.

Ahead, silhouetted atop the hill, he could see Chloe banging on his sign with a hammer. He broke into a run.

"What are you doing to my sign?" he shouted, breathless, scrabbling up the hill.

Like a child who will not cry over a scraped knee until the arrival of his mother, the sign refused to show any weakness until Milton showed up. Then, it promptly plopped facedown into the dirt.

"My sign!" said Milton.

"It was going to get us caught," Chloe said, letting the hammer fall at her side. "The posters. Our name."

Then she explained to Milton how the Milkhammer twins were blackmailing them. Brad and Erica had taken the posters down at school, and were the only ones who knew both Milton and Chloe's names and their faces. Unless they gave the Milkhammers a box of candy each, every day, the twins would call Mr. Porifera and have them carted back to the zipper factory at Urchin House.

"Unholy mackerel," said Milton. The two of them—most importantly, him—would have to give up eating Argyle's candy so that it would last as long as possible.

They walked back down the hill to the house. Chloe put up the hood of her sweatshirt against the evening chill.

The squampkin vines along the edge of the patch shuddered in the dusk, almost as if reaching out for the Nasselrogt children. *Funny,* Milton thought. Because the wind did not seem to be blowing that hard.

Weeks of anxious days passed.

Milton dragged his sign down into the basement, reluctantly storing his pride in the squampkin patch among the dusty jars of pumpkin butter.

Walking back across the basement toward the stairs, his foot caught in a hole in the middle of the floor, sending him flopping to the ground like a beaver's tail.

Milton pushed himself up onto his hands and knees and turned around. It was some kind of drainage hole, about three inches across and black as a pot of ink. Looking down into it, Milton could feel a faint, dank breeze wafting up against his face.

He fished a penny from his pocket, held it over the center of the hole, and let it drop. The penny vanished into darkness. Milton waited and listened.

Seconds passed. Milton strained his ears, and began to hear a faint, guttural purr from deep in the hole, like a simmering coffee-pot or a very sick kitten.

He pushed himself to his feet, trying to shake the idea that the bottomless pit in the basement could have anything to do with Charlie Argyle's disappearance.

Again, the doorknob at the top of the stairs came off in his hand, and again he was forced to call out to Chloe to open the door and let him in.

Helsabeck continued to watch from the bay window of his house across the street.

"You know, I think he's watching the squampkin patch," Chloe said.

"Why's that?" asked Milton.

Chloe shrugged.

"His name is Mr. Helsabeck," said Milton. "The terrible twins' mom told me."

"Like in the 'Pumpkin/Chocolate' journal," Chloe said.

Milton nodded. "The same," he said.

At the end of every school day, minutes after the passing of the yellow bus, the twin Milkhammers would stumble up through the squampkin patch and knock on the Nasselrogts' door.

Milton and Chloe took turns handing over the day's blackmail payment of candy. Chloe was especially sensitive to the Milkhammers' nearly superhuman guilt-making abilities. Milton was especially sensitive to the fact that candy was no longer the staple that held together his diet. If it had not been for the sugar boulder in the kitchen, he may very well have lost his reason.

He considered it an unnecessarily cruel irony that it was his turn to hand the twins the box that contained the last of his favorite candy, the peanut-butter cups. Argyle had used a particularly brittle dark chocolate for the shell, which did wonders to accentuate the grainy sweetness of the peanut butter.

Both twins, as usual, were grinning as they accepted the boxes. But this time, the leftmost twin, as soon as the box was in hand, began to giggle maniacally, a high-pitched sound like a mouse with its nose caught against an electric fan: "Hehehehehehehehehehe!" Along with the giggling, the twin's eyes had stopped agreeing on which way to focus, and were wandering around in strange, independent orbits.

"Peanut butter!" said the other twin.

"What?" said Milton, shouting over the high-pitched giggling.

"Hehehehehe . . . I'm . . . hehehehe . . . I'm allergic! Hehehe-hehehehe!" said the twin.

"To peanuts?" asked Milton.

"No," said the exasperated Milkhammer whose eyes still pointed in the same direction. "To peanut butter."

The giggling twin dropped the box of candy. Milton leaned down and pulled out one of the small, crown-shaped chocolates.

"It's a peanut-butter cup," he said.

"HEHEHEHEHEHEHEHEHEHEHEHEHE!" the allergic twin said, on the verge of collapse, eyes spinning.

The other twin slapped the candy from Milton's hand, crushed it underfoot on the porch, then stamped on the box of remaining peanut-butter cups as if extinguishing it. Both twins, one moving like a broken marionette, turned and hurried back home.

Milton stared at the crushed peanut-butter cups on the porch. The impression of the Milkhammer's sole was clearly visible in the smashed mound of chocolate. But it still looked delicious. . . .

"Don't do it," said Chloe from the hallway behind him.

"Don't do what?" said Milton, wiping the drool from the corner of his mouth.

They conserved their quickly dwindling candy supply to keep the Milkhammers from phoning Porifera. Chloe and Milton spread out the remaining candy among as many boxes as possible, but they would still run out soon.

"It's not our candy anyway," said Chloe, trying to reason with her brother. "We don't deserve it any more than the Milkhammers do."

Milton did not answer, but his stomach asked, "Grumble, grumble, gurgle?"

Chloe did not have an answer for that one.

Even worse, Milton and Chloe could tell that the Milkhammer twins savored the Nasselrogts' reluctance to hand over the candy as much as the taste of the candy itself.

Chloe chipped at the sugar boulder nightly for reading light, and Milton licked the thing constantly, but it showed no sign of dwindling.

Milton took comfort in his squampkin patch. Each morning, he woke to find the gourds noticeably larger. They were now the size of cantaloupes, and still covered in dark-green veins. What little orange of the rind showed through nearly glowed. The squampkins could have been candles in cast-iron latticework globes.

While watering the squampkin patch in the mornings, Milton would watch Margery Milkhammer jog by. He wrestled with the idea of telling her that her children were blackmailers, but was always restrained by the fact that it would almost certainly result in a phone call to Porifera.

The weather grew colder, and the trees shed the last of their leaves. The sky was gray, but comforting, like a careworn sweater.

Milton and Chloe watched the neighborhood children ride their bikes through streets carpeted in dry leaves. They ached at the memory of wheels crunching over orange and brown, scarves fluttering behind, movement so near to flight that it was difficult not to release the handlebars and try to hug the world rushing toward you.

Walking to and from town, they saw fathers throwing footballs with their children. They watched mothers forced to rake the same leaves together over and over again because their children could not resist leaping into the soft, crisp mounds.

"Halloween's in a few weeks," said Chloe. A few houses already had pumpkins on their porches, though none had yet been carved into jack-o'-lanterns. "Are we going to go trick-or-treating?"

"Absolutely," said Milton, "but we're going to need costumes." There were only a dozen costumes on display at the drugstore, however, and none of them were really scary.

"Is your blood curdling?" Milton asked.

"Nope," said Chloe.

"I hope *something* scary happens this Halloween," Milton said.

It was Milton's turn to hand the Milkhammers their candy payment.

"Thank you," they said as one.

Milton nodded wearily and began to close the door.

"Just a moment." One of the Milkhammer twins peeked inside a box to make sure there were no peanut-butter cups lurking and said, "Ah, excellent. Pistachio divinity, my favorite."

"We really are lucky," said the other. "I thought we'd never see it again. Though I wouldn't say I miss Charlie Argyle."

"No, not in a million years."

"Nasty man."

"But his candy!"

"Marzipan truffles."

"Caramel creams."

"Chocolate turtles."

"Chocolate pistachio-butter cups."

"And the pastries."

"Grumble," said Milton's stomach.

"Yeah, absolutely," said Milton.

"What?" said a Milkhammer twin.

"Nothing," said Milton. "You were telling me about all the candy I don't get to eat anymore."

"Well, we had gotten onto pastries," said a twin.

"Almond croissants!" said the other.

"Chocolate croissants!"

"Macaroons."

"You know, I never liked the pumpkin chocolate-chip cookies," said the right-hand twin.

"They were kind of weird," agreed the other. "Too spicy."

"But the chocolate chocolate-chip cookies . . ."

"With chocolate on top?"

"That's what I'm talking about."

"I still dream about them," said the left-hand twin.

"I don't care how nasty Mr. Argyle was," said the other.

"Or creepy. He was getting creepier all the time."

"And meaner."

"And almost . . ." The Milkhammer Twins looked at each other and shuddered.

"But it was always worth it," said the right-hand twin. "Nothing is as good as the sweets he made."

"I could have put up with any cruelty for the macaroons."

"I thought they were lost to us forever."

"But now we've got you." Twin Milkhammers unleashed twin smiles on Milton.

"It won't last forever," said Milton. "We don't have that much candy left."

The twin smiles vanished.

"We only have ten boxes left." Milton counted them daily, miserable. "If you both keep taking boxes, then we'll run out. . . ."

While Milton counted days in his head, Chloe called out from the other room, "Wednesday."

"Thanks, Chloe," said Milton. "Wednesday."

The Milkhammers looked at each other, thinking.

"The night before Halloween," said one of them.

"A year to the day since Benny vanished," said the other.

"Benny?" said Milton.

"He disappeared a few weeks before Charlie Argyle did," whispered a twin, leaning forward conspiratorially.

"But who was Benny?" Milton asked.

Chloe emerged from the living room and stood in the doorway, watching.

One of the twins looked from Milton to Chloe. The other cast a backward glance at the avocado Helsabeck house across the street. Then their eyes found each other.

"We have to go," they said, nearly simultaneously.

They turned and hurried off the porch.

Milton shut the door, wishing he had thought to do it fast enough to hit the Milkhammers on their way out, and turned to Chloe.

"I wonder who Benny is," he said.

"Benny's in Argyle's journal," said Chloe. "He's a kid that Argyle hated. Benny liked candy."

"I like candy," Milton said.

"He says Benny *really* liked candy."

"Have you finished reading it yet?" asked Milton.

"No," said Chloe, "but I should."

And, but for the missing pages torn from the end, she did.

Chapter 18

The Pumpkin/Chocolate Trials,
June 28–October 10

The entries in the journal grew less frequent in the final pages leading up to the missing section, notes jotted between hastily scrawled recipes, planting diagrams, and sketches of seeds, ingredients, and cooking techniques.

By the light of a burning chip of sugar, Chloe read.

June 28

Horrible little children. Big little Benny especially. Horrible, horrible. Letter in the mail from Chef Rutley this afternoon, there is a pastry shop available on the Rue Pamplemouse in Paris. "Only $400,000," writes Rutley! Only!

First real contact from the Squash Underground. Got a letter from a man named GARDNER GRAY. Planting instructions for the squampkins. Says "sow your squampkins far enough from your home

that the tunnels will not threaten its foundation."
Never heard of tunneling gourds. Root structure
of the vines, maybe?

The squampkins are thriving in the patch.
Buckskins and Ghost Riders farther up the hill
growing more slowly.

Must escape, must buy my Parisian pastry
shop. Took me five years to save the $10,000 un-
der the bed. At that rate, two centuries before I
can buy my patisserie.

"It says the squampkins make tunnels," Chloe said. "That's
weird."

She could not tell if Milton was listening, and flipped ahead
through scribbles and notes to the next entry.

June 30

Benny maintains his vigil. My dedicated
drooler outside the shop window. I watch the
Milkhammer twins eating truffles right in front
of him. They've got Benny in tears. Maybe some
kids aren't all bad.

Started selling pumpkin chocolate-chip cookies
in the shop today. The kids like the orange color.
They want free samples, I tell them to take a walk.

They buy cookies, they grimace, they say "weird." Warms my heart.

Squampkin vines taking over the whole patch. Growing too fast. Strangling the pumpkins on the hill. Tried cutting them back, but the sap gummed up the saw and stank like death. Writing to M & R Ake, Inc. Writing to the Winter Squash Underground.

July 5

Free samples of pumpkin chocolate-chip cookies to adults, but still nobody is buying them.

Squampkin vines have strangled all the others. A letter from Mr. Gray—he'll be here in two days.

July 7

Sounds in the squampkin patch woke me last night. Saw a man standing in the vines. Short man, round belly, bald as a jellyfish. Could see gold teeth smiling and a shiny scalp gleaming in the moonlight.

Grabbed a rolling pin, ran into the yard. The man was gone. Nervous-making.

Caught Benny in my trash again behind the shop, mouth full of cookies. I threatened to bake him into a pie. I would, too, if only I weren't worried about the smell.

July 9

The man in the squampkin patch was Mr. Gray. Gardner Gray, of the Winter Squash Underground. Tells me I have an excellent squampkin patch. All of his teeth are gold. Moves like he's on puppet strings. Can't see Mr. Gray's eyes for the glare in his glasses, even in a dark room.

Gardner Gray is excited, tells me I've got the healthiest squampkin patch he's ever seen.

Here's the important part: Gray tells me the squampkins could make me RICH. Lots of malarkey about reaping and sowing. "What you seed, they harvest" and all kinds of nonsense. "Rich" was the only word I really heard.

Gardner Gray says that he'll need his cut. He'll tell me how to reap the squampkins, but only if I give him part of the harvest.

Before he left, Gray promised to return before the first full moon before Halloween. Curious.

"Somebody named Gardner Gray told Argyle that the squampkins could make him rich," Chloe said.

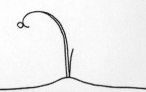

"Rich?" The word got Milton's attention. "How?"

"I'm not sure. It's all kind of creepy." Chloe kept reading.

August 17

My pastry shop is still infested with children. Could I put out truffle-baited traps? Maybe fumigate the place? Glue traps? God knows I've thought of poison.

I threw a cream puff at Benny this afternoon. Trying to chase him away from the shop. It bounced off his head, he didn't even twitch. The cream puff landed in the mud. He stared at it for a full five minutes before I looked away. I looked back, and the cream puff was gone. Benny was walking away, chewing.

Even the pumpkin chocolate-chip cookies couldn't persuade adults to come into the shop. I've stopped making them. Maybe for the best anyway. All my pumpkin vines are dead. The squampkins have taken over the whole field.

Nights, it almost seems I can hear the squampkin vines stir. Probably nerves. But I do wonder. How exactly will they make me rich?

I wait for Mr. Gray's return. Checked the almanac, the last full moon before Halloween is October 13.

August 26

An intruder! Got home from the shop and found child-size sneaker prints in the hallway of my house. How did he get inside? Can't find anything missing.

"Hmm," Chloe said, "there was somebody inside Argyle's house."
"What, a burglar?" asked Milton.
"I don't know."

August 28

The intruder was stealing candy! One piece missing from each of over two hundred boxes! How long has this been going on?

"Candy burglar," said Chloe.
Milton shuddered.

September 4

Nearly caught the intruder! I came home from the shop early. Heard a noise in the kitchen. Called out and heard glass shatter, scampering feet.
I ran to the kitchen, but he was gone. Broken

jar of pumpkin butter on the ground. I grabbed a rolling pin, searched the house. Somehow he escaped.

September 12

The little animals are back in their cages, school is back in session. The shop is mine again.

The squampkins are ugly. Dark green, heavy as lead. I look out at my field. Almost feels like they're watching me. How could they possibly make me rich?

September 25

The interloper is a clever little thief. I've been sneaking into my own house, hoping to catch him. Candy, pastries, jars of pumpkin butter—all go missing. My rolling pin is always with me. I'm ready.

"Did he catch the candy burglar yet?" Milton asked.
"No." Chloe said.

October 10

Received a letter from Gardner Gray! He'll be here tomorrow, or the next day.

The next page read "Octob . . . ," the word cut short by the torn edge of paper. At least a dozen pages were missing before the final entry, the first words Chloe had read from the "Pumpkin/Chocolate Trials":

October 31
     Helsabeck! He got to the patch before me! He must have sowed it with candy! His punishment . . .

"That's it," Chloe said. "It just ends."

"Kind of a weak ending," Milton said, yawning.

"There are pages missing," Chloe said. She knew her brother would think it foolish, so she did not say aloud the rest of what she was thinking:

Something very bad happened in the Argyle house.

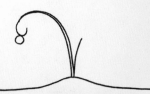

Chapter 19

Audience of Gourds

Halloween was approaching.

The squampkins were still growing.

Chloe sorted through Charlie Argyle's piles of books, recipes, magazines, and scraps, but could find no evidence of the pages missing from the "Pumpkin/Chocolate Trials."

Milton was winding himself tighter and tighter with excitement over selling squampkins. Chloe often found him wearing his new suit, posing before the mirror with a hand thrust Napoleonlike into the vest, or adjusting his tie so that the hula girl hung straight.

Hundreds of squampkins, now the size of basketballs, nested in the thick tangle of vines surrounding the house. They were a fierce orange beneath their webbing of green veins. The squampkins showed evidence of their pumpkin forefathers in their thick ridges; they were like tightly balled fists made entirely of thumbs, or spherical clusters of bananas.

The Nasselrogts had only six boxes of candy left.

"We have to figure out what we're going to do when we run out," said Milton. He and Chloe stood over a train wreck of pots and pans filled with clotted chocolate, burnt butter, and cashews that looked like they were returning from a trip through a sick cat. They had read Argyle's candy recipes and followed the instructions as closely as they could, but still their attempts to create his confections were a disaster.

They told the Milkhammer twins repeatedly that the candy was running low, but they might as well have been asking which one was Brad and which one Erica.

"How do we keep them from calling Porifera?" Milton mused aloud.

"Maybe they'll decide to be nice," offered Chloe. "Or they'll just forget about it."

Milton raised his eyebrows and looked at Chloe.

"Yeah, right," she said, licking ruined chocolate from her fingers.

"We could dig a tiger pit in front of the porch. Maybe put some spikes in the bottom," Milton said.

"We could use Argyle's money to buy candy at the grocery store." Chloe knew her brother well enough not to even respond to his spiked pit idea.

"No. Plastic-bag candy is sugared poo compared to Argyle's. The Milkhammers would catch on." Milton poured burnt butter into the garbage. "I think there's a shovel in the basement. One of

us could dig while the other one sharpens sticks . . ."

"We're not digging a tiger pit," interrupted Chloe.

There was a knock on the door.

"They're early," Milton said. "Whose turn is it to talk to them?"

"Yours," said Chloe, pushing two boxes of candy into Milton's hands. He never would have imagined that the act of receiving candy could have pained him so.

The twin Milkhammers were worse than early. They were their mother.

Margery Milkhammer stood sternly on the stoop. Her eyes were even narrower than usual; falling under that gaze felt to Milton like finding himself beneath a drill powered by discomfort. For once, Margery Milkhammer's voice matched her looks.

"Have you been giving my Brad and Erica candy?" she asked.

Milton looked down at the two boxes in his hands.

"They haven't eaten dinner in three weeks!" Margery said. "I took them to the dentist yesterday, and they had seven cavities between them! They're getting chubby ankles!"

Milton looked down. His own ankles had thinned considerably. He smiled.

"What are you smiling at?" Margery snapped.

"Sorry," Milton said.

"Is this how you think you're going to make friends?" Margery asked, tapping the candy boxes.

"What?" said Milton.

"I can understand wanting Brad and Erica to like you; they're wonderful. But you can't buy friends with candy."

Margery's logic was so far offtrack that Milton was struck speechless. Number one: The idea of trying to make friends with Brad and Erica was as strange to him as, say, trying to brush your teeth with a scorpion. Number two: Of course you could make friends with candy.

Margery interrupted his chain of thought before Milton could get to number three. "If you want a playdate with my kids, you and your sister can just come by the house. We'll make bean art," she said.

"Um," said Milton.

"But stop giving them candy!" Margery pointed at Milton. "My kids don't need that junk, so it ends here and now."

"But what if they come by and want more?" Chloe asked from the kitchen doorway. Margery's eyes darted like a fencer's lance toward Milton's sister.

"Don't give my kids any more candy," Margery said. "Period."

"But what do we do if they come back asking? Question mark," Milton said.

"Don't try to blame my kids for your own mistake. Bullies always try to blame the victim. When your Uncle Charlie gets back in town, he'll hear about this." Margery wagged her finger between Milton and Chloe.

She turned to leave, and Milton started to close the door. Then Margery stopped, spun, and grabbed the boxes of candy from Milton's hands.

Milton gasped as Margery Milkhammer turned again and marched with the candy into the squampkin patch. The door shut.

Milton and Chloe watched Margery through the front windows as she stalked home, digging into the candy boxes and shoveling the sweets into her mouth.

"Is this good news or bad news?" asked Chloe.

"The way things have been going for us," said Milton, "I would guess bad news."

"Will they call Porifera?" Chloe asked.

"I don't know," Milton said. "We should have dug a tiger pit a long time ago."

Chloe almost nodded. Then she frowned, thinking.

"Are they getting closer?" she asked.

"What?"

"The squampkins."

Milton looked at the patch. "No, they're just getting bigger, so it looks like they're closer."

"It really looks like they're closer," said Chloe.

The squampkins in the patch suddenly seemed like an attentive audience of gourds, the orange-and-green rinds all facing the Nasselrogt children.

"I think," said Milton, his voice showing its first glimmer of pride in weeks, "that it's about time to sell some squampkins."

Chloe looked over at Milton. His ears were wiggling. Something had his brain spinning faster than gourd sales could account for. Candy.

They had four boxes of uncommitted Argyle confections in the kitchen that needed attending to. After weeks of self-denial, hungrily watching the Milkhammer twins gobble down Argyle's stocks, Milton felt like he'd dunked his head in a bucket of paradise when he popped the first chocolate into his mouth.

"What about Porifera?" Chloe asked. "Where do we go if the Milkhammers call him?"

Milton shook his head and shrugged, chewing.

Chloe sighed, grabbed a box of candy, and popped a caramel-cashew chocolate turtle into her mouth.

Milton repainted the amputee coffee table as he ate his second box of candy. By the time he had scarfed down the last truffle, the sign had been changed to read SQUAMPKINS FOR SALE.

The rediscovery of candy and Milton's satisfaction with the new sign combined to create a dangerously effervescent cocktail of joy. He lay on the ground and spun in a circle until his glee was manageable.

Milton took the sign, a hammer, and nails out to the box elder and again pounded on the sign until it gave up and agreed to stay put.

He stepped back into the squampkin patch and grinned at his sign. All around him, the great gourds sat fat and satisfied in their tangle of vines.

There was a rustling, and a wave of dizziness swept over Milton, as if the earth had tilted. It felt as though all of the hundreds of squampkins, at once, had leaned slightly toward the house. Milton shook his head to clear some of the sugar haze, and told himself to ease more slowly into his next candy binge.

Milton turned and saw Chloe standing on the front porch. He waved, still grinning.

"You think this sign'll get us into trouble?" he asked.

Chloe pondered the sign, trying to connect the squampkin patch with Charlie Argyle's cryptic warnings about the dangers of mysterious squash. But her brother's enthusiasm overpowered her, and she grinned and shook her head. "No, I like it."

If Milton's own grin had widened any farther, the top half of his head might have slid off.

"I'm going into town," Milton said.

"What for?"

"I've got to plant some seeds," he answered, ears a-wiggle.

"What kind of seeds?" Chloe asked.

"Hanker seeds," said Milton, wishing he had farmerlike suspenders to hook his thumbs into. "I'm not sure this town knows it has a hankering for squampkins yet."

It reminded Chloe of the line scrawled on the back of Gardner Gray's card: *What you sow, they will reap.*

* * *

Milton put on his suit and clipped on his hula-girl tie. He looked at himself in the mirror, hooking his thumbs into his vest.

"That," he said, "is a man you want to buy squampkins from."

As he was walking into town, Milton glanced up into the window of a passing school bus and met the eyes of the Milkhammer twins, on their way home.

Milton thought of all the candy he had eaten that afternoon, smiled, and waved. The Milkhammers did not wave back.

There were five places in town selling pumpkins for Halloween. Milton went to each and hung around talking with the merchants, showing off the knowledge he had picked up from Charlie Argyle's jars of pumpkin butter.

"That's a nice-looking Ghost Rider," he would say, "but your Dickinson Munchkins are a little on the chubby side."

Once a good-size crowd had gathered, Milton would casually say, "Well, these are all very nice, but tell me, do you have any *squampkins?*"

Nobody, of course, did. Milton would act shocked.

"But it's not Halloween without squampkins!" he would say.

When he reached the fifth store, he found taped to the front window a handwritten sign that read SORRY, NO SQUAMPKINS. Milton grinned, his work was done here. He headed back to the Argyle house to wait for the customers to roll in.

* * *

"Well, it's really more my brother's squampkin patch than mine," Chloe said. "Can you wait for him?"

"Sure, sure," Mr. Fedora said. His name was not really "Mr. Fedora," which would have been a little ridiculous. Chloe had merely begun to think of him by that name because he wore such a nice hat.

Mr. Fedora's family, along with two others, were strolling through the squampkin patch, fascinated, admiring the gourds. Fathers and mothers walked arm in arm to ward off the chill, leaning into each others' warmth, and smiling. Children ran laughing through the vines, not caring how frequently they tripped and tumbled.

Chloe, in her red hooded sweatshirt, watched with a smile and a lump in her throat. The only thing she missed more than her parents was her *family*.

She turned away, and found herself looking at the figure in the window of the avocado house across the street. *Mr. Helsabeck*, Milton had said his name was. Chloe was bored with being intimidated by him. She raised a hand and waved.

Mr. Helsabeck's hand twitched, and then he was still. He and Chloe watched each other for several seconds, then he pulled back from the window and vanished.

For the first time, Chloe thought that perhaps Mr. Helsabeck was more sad than scary. A stick-figure seagull creased her forehead as she tried to piece together the evidence from the house, the "Pumpkin/Chocolate Trials," and the Milkhammers' gossip.

*Charlie Argyle's disappearance, Gardner Gray, Mr. Helsabeck, Benny's
disappearance, M & R Ake, Inc., the danger of squampkins. And who
was Benny . . . ?*

She had nestled so deep into these thoughts that Milton's voice
made her jump like she was being ejected from a toaster.

"Who are all these people?" Milton asked.

"Customers," said Chloe.

Now Milton grinned so wide that the top of his head *did* slide
off. Chloe wiped the dirt off of it and screwed it back on.

"Though none of our neighbors have come," she said, "It's all
people from town." Indeed, the few joggers and dog walkers who
had passed and seen the squampkin sale had hurried onward as if
trying to get home before a storm.

Milton was too excited to respond. He rubbed his hands together and ran over to Mr. Fedora.

"Good afternoon, sir." Milton said. "Happy Halloween."

"Why, hello there, little man. Happy Halloween." Mr. Fedora
tipped the front of his hat back with his thumb. "Nice suit."

"Is there anything I can help you with?" Milton asked.

"The kids are pretty excited about getting a squampkin," said
the man.

"Ah, squampkins. Let's see . . ." Milton turned and looked
around at the nearly two hundred gourds nestled in their vines.
"Squampkins we have."

"This one! This one!" said a little blond boy and a little blonde

girl, the Fedora children, jumping up and down over one of the larger squampkins in the field.

"Well, then," said Mr. Fedora. "Looks like you've got yourself a sale. What's the damage?"

"The damage?" said Milton.

"How much for the squampkin?"

Milton's grin did not fade at all, but the mirth in his eyes was replaced by a moment's panic. He had not considered the idea of actually taking money for the gourds. He said the first number that came into his head.

"Fifty-seven . . ." And after some more thought, he added, "Dollars."

Mr. Fedora whistled.

"Squamp-kin! Squamp-kin! Squamp-kin!" chanted the little Fedoras.

Mr. Fedora looked in his wallet with tented eyebrows, thumbed through some bills, and then grinned.

"Kid, you've got yourself a deal," he said.

"Mister, you got yourself a squampkin," Milton said, trying to sound like a farmer. "Just let me get something to cut the stem with."

Milton ran through the patch toward the house. *Fifty-seven dollars!* He was going to be rich.

"Excuse me!" another father called out. "Are you who we talk to about buying four of these wonderful gourds?"

"Absolutely!" shouted Milton. "I'll be with you in just a moment." A vine caught his ankle and Milton cartwheeled into the earth.

He got up, grinning, brushed the dirt off of his suit, and sprinted into the house.

He emerged moments later with a bread knife. Chloe watched him lope between the vines toward the Fedora children, the knife's blade gleaming in the gray autumn afternoon. She wished she was his *older* sister so that she could tell him not to do something as stupid as running with a bread knife.

"This one?" Milton asked, panting for breath.

"Squamp-kin! Squamp-kin!" said the Fedora children.

"This one," said Mr. Fedora.

Milton smiled and kneeled down over the gourd. It was the size of a beach ball, and too large for Milton to lift alone. A few strands of dark-green veins still webbed its surface, but, by and large, the rind was the fierce orange of dramatically overtanned parents.

Milton grabbed the thick, dark squampkin vine and put the bread knife to it.

"You may want to stand back," Milton said to the Fedora kids. Mr. Fedora put a hand on each of their shoulders; all three of them smiled down at Milton.

Milton firmly grasped the vine, positioned the blade a few inches above the squampkin, and began to saw. He grunted and puffed, making little progress until the fourth stroke, when the

toothed blade abruptly ripped into the woody stem.

A stench like the community showers in an old-goats' home erupted from the gourd. The bread knife tore through the rest of the vine, severing the squampkin.

"Gah!" said Milton, as the smell from the cut vine grabbed him by the ears and began kicking him in the face.

The Fedoras stepped back, repulsed by the odor.

Chloe watched them, that stick-figure seagull back on her forehead.

A chorus of distant barks and howls rose from the neighborhood. Chloe looked up and down the street. Every dog on the block was going crazy.

The smell knocked Milton back onto his butt; he dropped the bread knife and scooted away from the gourd. It smelled like somebody was slow-roasting toads stuffed with Gorgonzola cheese.

Black sap oozed from both ends of the cut vine. The thick, tarlike goo seeped out of the stem and over the squampkin, pooling at its base.

"It smells like grandma!" said one of the Fedora children.

"And it's leaking like grandpa!" said the other.[5]

"What do you kids think about a pumpkin instead?" asked Mr. Fedora.

The Fedora kids nodded desperately. Mr. Fedora offered Milton

---

5 Grandpa Fedora was a smoker. Kids, don't smoke.

an apologetic grin, then ran with his children back to their car.

The other few families escaped into their own automobiles. A dozen tires squealed, and the cars all diminished back toward town and its more traditional pumpkin merchants.

Milton looked at the cut squampkin. It was noticeably withering, collapsing in on itself—a pretty good imitation of how Milton felt.

Within moments, it was little more than a dark, malodorous stain on the ground. And then it was gone.

Chapter 20

The Glare of the Naked

Milton tried cutting into two other squampkins to make sure he had not just chanced onto a rotten gourd, but they all stunk like curdled corpses and oozed black sludge.

Dozens of families, potential customers, pulled up to the Argyle house, got out of their cars, sniffed, then got back into their cars and drove away.

Milton tried to clear the smell from the patch with the garden hose, but it was like making curdled-corpse soup: It only strengthened the smell.

Milton gave up and dropped the hose on the porch, walking back into the house. The spray nozzle hissed and sputtered, leaking water onto the paint-flaked wood.

He showered for an hour, scrubbing his way through all the soap in the house, but was not able to get rid of the stink on his hands. The stench made dinner difficult to stomach, and Milton ended the day hungry, disappointed, and tired.

* * *

"I'm sorry your squampkin patch smells like evil," Chloe said.

Milton nodded but did not answer. He was looking across the street at the avocado house, where the empty front window glowed. It was nearly midnight.

"I don't think it's safe to stay here," said Chloe. "Porifera's posters, and the Milkhammer twins, and . . ." She almost said *the squampkins*, but again could not imagine what, exactly, was dangerous about them.

"We'll figure it out tomorrow," said Milton. "I don't want to worry about taking care of you right now."

Milton lay back on the sofa, still wearing his suit, and shut his eyes. Chloe lay down on her nest of blankets on the floor and closed her eyes too. A few minutes later, and no closer to sleep, she propped herself up on one elbow.

"We haven't even thought about costumes," Chloe said.

"What?" murmured Milton.

"Halloween's the day after tomorrow."

Milton grumbled something meaningless, already past the midway point of sleep. After a few minutes, Chloe began to softly snore.

Tappity tappity tappity tappity tap.

The sound of mice clog-dancing on glass woke Chloe. She popped to her feet. It was after midnight. Milton was gone from the sofa.

Something, no more than a dark shape, was tapping on the window. *Tappity tappity tap.*

"Milton," Chloe whispered.

"Over here," Milton said.

Milton was standing by the front door, his hand on the light switch. He flipped it on, and the porch light revealed the Milkhammer twins, who grinned and squinted against the glare of the naked bulb.

Milton and Chloe met them at the front door.

"Good evening," said half of the twins.

Milton and Chloe believed only the "evening" part of that phrase.

"What are you doing here?" Milton asked.

"Collecting our due," said a twin.

"We'll have to come under cover of darkness from now on," said the other. "Our mother thinks candy isn't good for us."

The twins clucked their tongues and shook their heads.

Milton and Chloe looked at each other. Milton was trying to wiggle his ears, but no ideas came.

"So," said a twin. "Our due."

"Your doo?" said Milton.

"Our candy," said one twin, as the other used a sleeve corner to dab at drool.

"The candy's gone," said Milton.

The Milkhammer twins tried to look like they were disappointed, but their eyes gleamed like fishhooks.

"No more candy?" asked a twin.

"Oh dear," said the other.

"That wasn't very responsible of you."

"Not at all. In fact, it seems like the kind of thing a *fugitive* would do."

"Definitely," said the first Milkhammer. "Not responsible at all. In fact, I'm not sure the two of you are responsible enough to take care of yourselves."

"It might be safer for you back at the orphanage," said the second.

"The kindest thing we could do is call Mr. Porifera."

"Why are you so mean to us?" asked Chloe.

The Milkhammers froze in mid-sentence and pivoted slowly to look at Chloe. Each twin stared at one of Chloe's eyes until she dropped her gaze.

"What are you and Milton dressing as for Halloween?" one of them asked.

"What?" said Milton.

"What are your costumes?" asked the other twin.

"We hadn't thought of that yet. . . ."

Once again, the twins shook their heads and clucked their tongues.

"You could go as a banker," one of the twins said to Milton, looking at his three-piece suit.

"But you," said the other, to Chloe, "just look like a fugitive orphan."

"The day after tomorrow is Halloween," said the first twin.

"Get some costumes," said the second. "Go trick-or-treating."

"We'll meet you here at night's end, and collect what we missed tonight and tomorrow," said the first, again wiping at drool with a sleeve.

The Milkhammers and the Nasselrogts looked at one another over the Argyle threshold for several moments.

"Your pumpkin patch smells terrible," said a Milkhammer.

"They're squampkins," said Milton, quietly.

"You sound like you've grown attached to them," said the other Milkhammer.

"Don't get *too* attached," said the first. "Especially if you don't have any candy to hand out."

"Last year, Mr. Argyle didn't have any treats, so he got tricked."

"Those kids took it out on his pumpkin pa—"

"His *squampkin* patch," the second interrupted the first.

"What kids?" asked Milton.

"I don't know," said a Milkhammer. "Nobody saw them."

"But they dragged all those squampkins over into Mr. Helsabeck's yard," said the other.

"And then stole them."

"They were gone in the morning."

"It was a mess."

"And it smelled terrible."

"All the adults thought it was 'cause of a ruptured septic tank."

"But if you sniffed the vines you could tell it was his pumpk—"

"*Squampkin.*"

"His squampkin patch."

The Milkhammers wrinkled their noses at the memory. The action wrinkled their brains, reminding them that they were, in fact, now surrounded by the same stink.

"Good night," said one.

"Until Halloween," said the other.

Milton nearly closed the door fast enough to hit them on their way out, but not quite. *Next time,* he thought. He turned to Chloe.

"You know," he said, "if we had listened to me, we'd have the twins *and* their mom in a tiger pit right now."

Chloe was thinking about the squampkins dragged into Mr. Helsabeck's yard. She looked out of the front window at the Milkhammer twins slowly picking their way through the tangled vines in the darkness. One of them tripped. The other, trying to catch the first, fell on top.

It would have taken dozens of children several hours to move the entire patch into the yard across the street. Chloe glanced through a different window, looking up the hill at the great box elder, surrounded by hundreds more of the gourds.

The dark form of Mr. Helsabeck was creeping down the hill. The moonlight clearly illuminated, in his hand, a large ax.

Chloe felt the air rush out of her. In front of the house, the Milk-hammer twins were struggling to regain their feet in the tangle of vines.

Mr. Helsabeck was heading right for them.

Chloe tried to speak, her lips moving uselessly, her lungs refus-ing to draw air. Milton was still talking about his tiger pit.

"We could have stood on the edge and sprayed them with the hose until they told us which one was Brad and which one was Erica," he said.

"Hel . . . Hel . . ." Chloe could barely get the sound out. Her lungs felt utterly empty, even as her brain was filled with a rush of wind and noise.

Milton looked at her.

"Mind your language, Chloe," he said.

One of the Milkhammers was standing, trying to pull vines away from the other's legs. Helsabeck, the ax swinging at his side, crept steadily toward them.

A cry, somewhere between shock and fear, came from the Milk-hammer twins. Milton and Chloe's attention snapped over to them.

Helsabeck froze, ax poised.

"Helsabeck!" Chloe managed to hiss at Milton.

Milton followed his sister's eyes to the bottom of the hill, where Mr. Helsabeck raised the ax above his head, its crescent edge roughly gleaming as if newly sharpened, and ran at the Milkhammer twins.

The Milkhammers cried out again, now in real fear.

The world moved in nightmare time, creeping along like cold

molasses. Chloe's keen powers of observation were suddenly a curse. Every detail of Mr. Helsabeck, caught briefly in the moonlight, burned clearly into her brain—his pale skin, his limp hair, the look in his eyes wavering between panic and mania. And, most of all, that ax, drawn fully back and poised to swing, bobbing behind him as he ran toward the Milkhammers.

Brad and Erica were scrambling, screaming, pulling at the vines entangling them. The vines seemed to twist like snakes, taking firmer hold the harder the twins tried to pull away.

The thought of the gruesome details she would have to witness if Helsabeck's ax met the Milkhammers put Chloe in motion.

"Chloe! No!" Milton barely had time to shout before his sister was out the door and onto the porch.

"Stop!" Chloe shouted. "Stop! Stop!"

The Milkhammer twins looked up at her, eyes wide with fear, then back down at the vines holding them. Chloe realized suddenly that they were completely unaware of Helsabeck or his ax.

But Helsabeck was only feet away, taking the final step, ready to swing.

"No!" Chloe shouted.

Helsabeck's shadow fell over the Milkhammer twins, and they looked up at the towering, ax-wielding figure above them. They had only a moment's glimpse before Helsabeck drove the gleaming blade downward.

Chloe gasped and shut her eyes.

Dogs began to bark madly up and down the street.

A war cry erupted from behind her, then a sound like an enormous snake hissing and a splatter of water. The shout— "Yeaaaaaaargh!"—belonged to her brother. The hiss belonged to the garden hose.

Chloe opened her eyes just in time to see a stream of water arc across the squampkin patch and strike Helsabeck, who stood with his hands on the ax, the blade buried in the tangle of twins and vines at his feet.

Milton ran forward into the patch, holding the spray nozzle of the hose ahead of himself like a talisman.

The cold water splattered against Helsabeck's face. He lost his grip on the ax handle and spun away, stumbling through the squampkin patch toward the street.

Chloe's eyes helplessly sought out the sharp end of the ax, and into what it was buried. There was movement around it; at least one of the Milkhammer twins was struggling up and out of the soaked squampkin vines.

Milton kept the hose on Helsabeck, sending him tumbling out of the yard and into the street.

Chloe ran for the ax. She hopped between the vines, dodging the stream of water, which suddenly stopped.

"Chloe! Come back!" Milton shouted.

She ignored him, tottering as the thick woody tangle constricted around her running feet. She nearly fell, catching herself on the handle of the ax.

"Brad! Erica!" she called. They looked up at her from the ground, soaked and terrified, but seemingly unharmed. The ax had merely split an especially wide squampkin vine. Chloe wrenched it out, unleashing black ooze and a hideous stench. The vines shrunk back from around her ankles, and the Milkhammers scrabbled to their feet.

Mr. Helsabeck, soaking wet, had regained his feet as well. He stood in the street, panting.

The Milkhammers snapped into motion like slingshots, hustling out of the patch and sprinting for home.

Chloe looked up at Mr. Helsabeck. He was staring back at her, his face as pale as mayonnaise in the streetlight's glare. He was slack-jawed, limbs a-jangle, nose enormous, eyes terrified and tired. The wisps of hair he normally combed over his bald dome of a scalp were splayed like a rooster's crown above his head.

Helsabeck met Chloe's eyes only for a moment before his attention dropped to the squampkins at her feet. His eyes widened.

Chloe glanced downward, but before her eyes could focus on the gourds surrounding her, she was jerked into motion.

"Come on!" Milton hissed, dragging her roughly by the hand. She kept her grip on the ax, trailing it behind her as Milton pulled her toward the house, across the porch, and inside, then slammed the door.

He locked the doorknob, threw the deadbolt, hooked the chain, and then looked at Chloe, wild-eyed. He took a deep breath, then—

"Aaaaaaaaaaaaaaaaaahg!" he screamed, which seemed to make him feel better.

Chloe let the ax thump heavily onto the hallway floor.

Milton turned out the lights and ran to the front window just in time to see a wet Mr. Helsabeck duck back inside his own house.

For the moment, the Nasselrogt kids were safe.

Chapter 21

Relish Beyond Flabbergasted

Milton and Chloe sat in the darkened Argyle house until dawn, keeping a close watch on the avocado house across the street.

Between two and three in the morning, Helsabeck came to his front window and stared out.

"He can't see us, right?" said Milton. "We've got the lights out."

"We can see *him*, and he's got *his* lights out," said Chloe.

Milton drew a step back from the window.

"I think he's crying," whispered Chloe.

"You can't see him that well," Milton whispered back, only because he himself could not see Mr. Helsabeck that well. Chloe's sharp eyes could see the light of the street lamps shining off of Helsabeck's cheeks.

Neither of the Nasselrogt children had been willing to pick up Helsabeck's ax, so it lay where it had fallen in the hallway, black, malodorous goo dripping from the blade.

"We'll go to the police tomorrow," said Milton. "And then we're leaving Goodfellow's Landing."

"Good," said Chloe. "Where will we go?"

"I don't know," said Milton. "Somewhere without ax murderers. Canada, maybe."

Helsabeck drew back from the window and was swallowed by darkness, as if sinking into a tub of oil. The avocado house was so still it nearly seemed to vibrate, motionless around the vacated black window.

Chloe yawned. Outside, dead leaves swooped and skittered across the street and through the squampkin patch, tattered scraps of black against the streetlights. The squampkins seemed to quiver. Through the haze of her own sleep-deprived eyes, Chloe saw a dozen squampkins roll a quarter turn toward the house.

Chloe snapped out of near sleep and rubbed her eyes.

"I think . . ." she said, and then stopped. It was too ridiculous to say aloud.

"Did the squampkins just move?" Milton asked.

Chloe nodded.

As the night wore on, they grew accustomed to their fear. Exhaustion muffled the anxious beating of their hearts. They did not feel themselves falling into sleep until they were already slipping past the edge, and into the comforting hush of darkness.

Three hours later, the sun came up on Milton and Chloe curled asleep on the sofa in front of the window.

Milton blearily lifted his head, rubbed his eyes, and looked down at the silhouette of Gertrude Stein he had painted in drool on the cushion.

"Chloe, it's morning," he said.

There was no movement from the Helsabeck house, no dark figure in the front window. The dirt-speckled orange-and-green rinds of the squampkins rose from their tangled nest of vines.

Milton and Chloe walked the long way around the squampkin patch, staying well away from the vines.

"The Milkhammers," Chloe said. The twins were standing at the edge of the street in front of their house, backpack-clad. As soon as Milton and Chloe looked over, both Milkhammers developed a sudden interest in their shoelaces.

Milton and Chloe made a beeline for Brad and Erica.

"We're going to the police," Milton said. "Want to tag along?"

"No," said a twin.

"No?" asked Milton.

"We don't want to get into trouble," said the other Milkhammer.

"With whom?" asked Milton.

"Our mom."

"For sneaking out."

"Your mom?" Milton nearly shouted. "What about the guy who tried to chop you into quadruplets?"

"Who?" said a twin.

"Helsabeck!" said Milton.

"He saved us," said the other twin.

"We don't want to talk about it."

"Saved you from what?" asked Chloe.

"We don't want to talk about it."

Milton could still picture Mr. Helsabeck with the ax held above his head, ready to make Milkhammer relish. Beyond flabbergasted, Milton said, "He tried to chop you up! We're going to the police, and you should come with us."

"No," said one twin. "Mr. Helsabeck doesn't belong in jail."

"He wasn't attacking us," said the other. "He's not a bad man. He's just been sad since his son disappeared."

"What?" said Chloe. "His son?"

"Benito."

"Benny Helsabeck."

Chloe's mind spun so fast she nearly achieved liftoff.

Benny was Helsabeck's son.

Benny disappeared the night before Halloween, the night the neighborhood kids dragged Argyle's squampkin patch across the road, into Helsabeck's yard.

Argyle hated Benny, wanted him gone.

Benny loved candy.

The squampkins. Could the squampkins . . . move?

"What you sow, they will reap."

Benny Helsabeck.

"What . . . ? What . . . ?" Chloe's mind was clogged with questions. They all tried to step through the door of her mouth at the same time and got stuck, shoulder to shoulder.

A squeal like a cannon-shot piglet erupted behind her. The school bus noisily slowed to a stop and the doors swung open, revealing a familiar plaid-flannel-clad damsel behind the wheel.

"All aboard that's coming aboard," said the bus driver, pressing a large, homemade-looking green button on the bus's dashboard. The bus hissed and clanged, then hunkered down over its wheels so that the bottom of the bus scraped the ground and the bottommost step could be easily climbed.

"Beulah!" said Chloe.

The Milkhammer twins hurried onto the bus, vanishing into the crush of children shouting and spilling from their seats.

"Beulah!" said Milton.

Beulah squinted at them from the driver's seat, then said, "The digger kids! Why aren't you two in the coal mines?"

"Why aren't you driving the real bus?" asked Milton.

"You saying this ain't a real bus?" said Beulah.

"I meant the not-school bus," said Milton.

"That's just a summer job," said Beulah. "This is my real calling." She patted the steering wheel warmly and grinned down at the Nasselrogt children.

"You kids coming to school?" she asked.

"No," said Milton.

"Why not?"

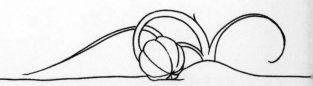

"We have to go to the police station," said Chloe.

"Our neighbor's an ax murderer," said Milton.

"Oh," said Beulah. "That *is* serious."

The bus's radio squawked and Beulah jumped as if it had poked her.

"Well, school waits, even if the tardy bell don't. I'll see you kids around?"

"Yeah," said Milton.

"Definitely," said Chloe.

Beulah extended a finger to the big green button, then winked at the Nasselrogts and said, "Pneumatics." She pressed the button and the bus hissed and clanged and rose back up over its wheels. Beulah shut the door and steered the screeching bus down the road.

"What do you think was wrong with her old matics?" Milton asked.

"She said 'pneumatics,'" Chloe explained, "not 'new matics.' It means a mechanical device powered by air. Like the thing that makes the bus go up and down."

"How do you know that?" Milton asked.

"Dad explained it to me," Chloe said. They were quiet for a few moments.

Milton and Chloe had to walk down the street between the squampkin patch and the Helsabeck house on their way to town. Neither was an inviting prospect, and they walked down the dead center of the road. Milton kept his eyes glued to the Helsabeck house. Chloe watched the squampkins.

"Paw prints," she said.

"What?"

"In the squampkin patch. Paw prints."

Milton looked over. There were indeed thumb-size indentations littering the squampkin patch.

"Maybe . . ." said Milton, "maybe puppies like squampkins."

Neither of them believed it. Somehow, it was easier to believe that maybe squampkins liked puppies.

Chloe had to stand on her toes to peek over the edge of the desk at the police station.

The receiving officer's name tag read HOGLICK. When he had been a child, the other children had been very cruel to him on account of his name. Even though he had aged, grown large, and earned a job where he was allowed to carry a gun and talk in code numbers, he still resented children.

"We'd like to report an ax murderer," said Milton.

"Marcy, we've got a number fourteen," Hoglick spoke into the phone on his desk, and then addressed the Nasselrogts. "Who got chopped up?"

"Nobody, yet," said Milton.

Hoglick scowled at Milton and Chloe, then picked up the phone and said, "Scratch that, Marcy—false alarm from some

overimaginative kids. We've only got a number sixteen."

"What's a number fifteen?" asked Chloe.

"Ax shoplifting," said Hoglick, narrowing his eyes at the children. "You look familiar," he said.

"I don't think we know you," said Milton.

"No . . ." Hoglick's eyes were like oyster knives, dull but prying. "But I've got an elephant's face for brains."

Milton and Chloe looked at him.

"I meant, an elephant's brain for a face."

Milton and Chloe looked at him.

"No, an elephant's brain for faces."

Chloe kicked Milton.

"Ouch," said Milton, and looked at his sister. She was making short, desperate, *Look over there* gestures with her head. Milton looked over there.

A FUGITIVE CHILDREN! poster stared back at him.

"What I meant was, I don't forget faces," said Hoglick. "And yours I've definitely seen before. But . . . not in three dimensions."

Milton's ears began to wiggle.

"We have to go," he said.

"What about this ax murderer?" asked Officer Hoglick.

"Tee-hee," said Milton. "That was our little joke."

"Tee-hee," said Chloe, not so convincingly.

"An early trick for Halloween," said Milton. "Means you don't have to give us treats. Come on, let's leave Officer Hoglick to his

job, uh"—Milton tried to come up with a fake name for his sister—
"Khloe."

"Wait," said Officer Hoglick.

Milton grabbed Chloe's hand and led her toward the exit. Hoglick
came around his desk.

"Wait a second," he said.

"We're late for school," said Milton. Barely shy of a run, he
dragged Chloe to the door. He grabbed the handle and pulled,
without effect. Officer Hoglick's much larger hand was pressed
against the door, holding it shut.

Milton looked up. Hoglick was looking at the FUGITIVE CHILDREN!
poster and grinning like a spider with a pair of flies in his parlor.

There were only two holding cells in the Goodfellow's Landing jail,
but Milton and Chloe were the only fugitives in town, so they each
got their own. The cells were side by side and separated by half a
foot of concrete. Milton and Chloe could not see each other, but
by reaching through the bars they could pass the time with bouts of
thumb wrestling (Milton always won) or rock-paper-scissors (Chloe
always won).

"I guess the orphanage is better than being chopped up," said
Milton.

"Yeah," said Chloe, distantly. Helsabeck and his ax had taken a
backseat in her mind to the squampkins. It was all too complicated,
and hopelessly grim.

Milton had spent some time trying to call out to Officer Hoglick from his cell and tell him more about Helsabeck and his ax, but Hoglick ignored him.

Hours passed. Milton tried to get Chloe to help him with an escape plan involving constructing fake moustaches from bars of soap and shoe polish, but Chloe would not say anything more than "Yeah" or "Nope."

Chloe's mind was so filled with thoughts of her lost parents, her ax-wielding neighbor, and dangerous squash that there was no brain-space left for conversation.

Milton and Chloe slept fitfully, and were awake on Halloween morning long before Hoglick brought in their breakfast brown-loaf.

"Brown-loaf!" said Milton. "Fancy running into you here."

"Squeak!" said the brown-loaf, in response to Milton's fork. Prison brown-loaf came with sickly sweet brown treacle. Chloe let Milton have her share of the stuff.

She was still too deep in thought to talk to Milton. A few hours after lunch, they began to hear the laughing voices of costumed children on the streets of Goodfellow's Landing.

"We're missing Halloween!" Milton said.

Chloe did not respond.

"This isn't fair! We could have been so scary!"

His sister still said nothing.

Milton reached his hand through the cell bars and around the cement wall that divided them. He patted her side of the wall.

"Are you there, Chloe?" he asked.

"Yeah," she said.

"Are you okay?"

"Nah," Chloe said. She took his hand and sat back against the wall.

That was how they were sitting when Porifera walked in.

Chapter 22

Rustling the Crinkle

Poor Porifera! **he had thought.** He had been spending hours of every day behind his desk, stewing in the juices of his worry for the fugitive Nasselrogts and his own misfortune. Poor, poor, Porifera.

Since Mr. and Ms. Nasselrogt had stopped phoning and pestering him about their missing children, his worry had only grown, swelling like a tick on an artery. The fear of having his incompetence exposed was constant, an anxiety he filed under "Things That Keep Poor Porifera Awake at Night."

What if the children were in danger? What if something had already happened to them?

Weeks—no, months had passed since Milton and Chloe had escaped.

On Porifera's orders, his assistants had dressed the orphans in the zipper factory in clown masks to celebrate Halloween, but even that had not lifted his mood.

In fact, he could barely lift anything, so deeply submerged was the world in the bitter molasses of despair.

When the phone rang, it took nearly all of Porifera's strength to pull the receiver from its cradle.

He listened to the voice on the other end, and a look dangerously close to hope flitted across his face. A few seconds later, for the first time in weeks, Porifera smiled.

"Thank you, Officer Hoglick," he said. "Thank you very much indeed."

Children who still had parents always gave Porifera the creeps. It did not help that they were dressed as goblins, superheroes, and the undead, dragging their sacks of candy through the purple autumn dusk.

All of his FUGITIVE CHILDREN! posters were gone. If Porifera had not had such sensitive toes, he would have kicked himself. Had he simply checked, the missing posters would have been a sure sign of the Nasselrogt children's residence in Goodfellow's Landing.

But he had them now. Before the sinking of Halloween's moon, he would have Milton and Chloe back in Urchin House, and this time he would zip them up for good.

Milton woke to find Porifera grinning at him through the bars of his cell. Pinching himself seemed like a foolish way to test whether or not he was in the middle of a nightmare, so he reached around the wall and pinched Chloe instead.

Both of them woke up, suddenly in their own beds. Porifera melted away, like any other nightmare's shadow, and they got out of bed and ran into the kitchen, where their parents were making banana pancakes!

That was another lie.

What really happened is that Chloe said "Ouch." Then Milton and Chloe Nassalrogt were released from prison, and returned to Porifera's possession.

Ka-chunk said the locks on Porifera's khaki sedan with the heavy finality of a coffin lid dropping into place. Just the same, Milton tried the door handle every time the car came to a stoplight.

Chloe still was not talking. She stared out of her window at the passing darkness, the sheeted ghosts, the painted witches, the masked goblins and ghouls, the dozens of Goodfellow's Landing children she had never met. They tricked and treated, traipsing along the lamp-lit suburban streets holding pillowcases heavy with sweets.

Porifera drummed his hands against the steering wheel to the cadence of a song of victory. *File all my problems under "Solved"* was the refrain. He had only to wipe every trace of the Nasselrogt children from this saccharine little town, and get them back to Urchin House.

The boy, Milton, had told obvious lies in response to all of his questions. Porifera had not believed for a moment that Milton and Chloe had performed a Martian mind-switch with a pair of twins who should now be taken to Urchin House in their place.

But the girl had been more reasonable. Chloe, in short, quiet words, had answered Porifera's every question.

All of their belongings were in a place they called "the Argyle house." They had not gone to school, nor had they interacted with any but a few of their neighbors.

Once Porifera had taken them through this Argyle house and collected their belongings, it would be as if Milton and Chloe had never come to Goodfellow's Landing at all.

A lemon-wedge moon hung bright behind motionless strips of torn cloud. Behind the Argyle house, the great box elder stood photograph-still, casting intricate shadows onto the simmering orange-and-green rinds of the squampkins. The flesh of the gourds rippled beneath the thick rind like the muscles of a sleeping cat.

Porifera ushered Milton and Chloe from the car, keeping anemone-like hands draped over their shoulders. The night was so still that the few straggling trick-or-treaters, blocks away, could be heard laughing and talking.

Porifera steered the Nasselrogt children toward the front porch, straight through the squampkin patch.

"Let's go around," said Chloe.

"We shouldn't walk through the patch," said Milton.

"Don't be ridiculous," said Porifera, pushing them forward through the vines. He was eager to collect the evidence and be gone.

Chloe stumbled so frequently on vines that Milton began to wonder if she were up to something. But he could not catch her eye; she was staring down at the hundreds of squampkins all around them.

There was a rustling across the entire patch—the crinkle of leaves, twigs scraping against earth.

Porifera shuddered with an imagined chill, a response to the breeze that must have stirred the patch. Milton and Chloe shuddered as well, because they knew there had been no breeze at all.

Chloe's hopelessness was infectious. Milton could feel it nibbling at him like a pack of flatulent marmots, surrounding him in a terrible funk as they nibbled away at his hope with tiny, quick teeth.

He watched Chloe shuffle through the house, gathering her few belongings. Her eyes shone like they did when she was trying not to cry. She had put on her red hooded sweatshirt, and now pulled the drawstrings on the hood so that her face peeked out of the smallest possible space. She walked heavily through the Argyle house, barely able to bear the weight of Porifera's scrutiny.

The Urchin House overlord watched them, grinning and rubbing his hands, wishing he had a mustache to twirl.

"Chop, chop, children," he said. "We can still make it to Urchin House before dawn."

"I'm done," said Chloe, nodding.

She looks done, thought Milton. *You probably could stick a cake tester in her without hearing any complaint.*

"Excellent. And you?" Porifera swung his head around on its improbable neck to face Milton.

Milton was wearing his three-piece suit and orange scarf, and could think of nothing else to collect. He began to nod, nearly giving in to the farting marmots of hopelessness, but that small dip of the head kick-started his ears. They gave a faint wiggle.

"Almost. Chloe, I forgot about the sign we made," Milton said.

"The sign?" Porifera asked.

Milton was trying to catch Chloe's attention, but her eyes would not even admit they were being chased. Through the puckered opening of her sweatshirt hood, Milton could see tears on her cheeks.

"The 'Nasselrogt Patch' sign," said Milton, very slowly, digging at Chloe with his eyes. She remained staring at the floor; she could have been sleepwalking.

"You put your name on a sign?" asked Porifera. "Where?"

"In the basement. I can go get it," said Milton. Then he added, "I can go by myself—it's no problem."

"By yourself?" said Porifera, barely able to keep his eyebrows on his head. "I don't think that's in your best interest. I'll come along."

Milton was shooting "Hey you" eye-lasers at Chloe, but she refused to lift her gaze from the floor. She might as well have been back on the assembly line at the zipper factory.

There was, faintly, a sound like a watermelon cracking open in the front yard. Chloe's attention leaped toward it. She stared through the front window at the squampkin patch beyond.

Milton's ears wiggled so furiously that they nearly brushed Porifera's limp hand off of his shoulder. He simply could not get Chloe's attention. Milton's plan was already pecking at its shell, and Chloe needed to be ready to act when it hatched.

But Chloe's eyes were locked on the front window. Milton, for his own rapid ear movement, could not hear the sound, like dozens, maybe hundreds, of gourds cracking open, the rainlike patter of loosened dirt falling to the ground. Beyond the darkness of the window, surrounding the house, the whole patch was coming to life.

Milton led Porifera to the basement door, casting one more glance over his shoulder at Chloe. He hoped desperately that she would be able to snap out of her funk.

He opened the door to the dark stairs sinking below the house. Milton needed Porifera to walk down the stairs ahead of him.

"I can go first," he said, stepping forward. Porifera's hand tightened on his shoulder.

"No. I'll go," said Porifera, suspicious of the boy.

"We're going into the basement, Chloe," said Milton. Chloe finally shot Milton a small glance. He added, "Hang *loose*, we can handle it."

Loose, thought Milton. *Handle it. Work with me, Chloe.*

She gave her brother no indication that she understood, but only turned back to the front window, where the darkness obscured the source of the crunching and dragging noises slowly building outside.

"Chop, chop," said Porifera, already on the first step.

"Okay," said Milton. He took a deep breath, grabbed the loose doorknob, and stepped forward onto the basement stairs, pulling the door shut behind him.

"Don't, it's too . . ." But before Porifera could say "dark," Milton had slammed the door, yanking the loose knob off of its spindle.

Milton and Porifera were cast into a darkness as absolute as an inkwell's.

"Run, Chloe!" Milton shouted through the heavy door. "Run! Run!"

Pitched into blackness, Milton felt Porifera's hands fumble past him, trying to find the doorknob. Milton dodged sideways, grabbing hold of the stair rail.

As Porifera muttered and fumbled at the knobless door, Milton clumped clumsily down the dark stairs.

"Run!" he shouted again. "Run, Chloe!"

There was no way to tell whether or not she was taking the opportunity to escape. Milton forgot that the banister ended on the fourth step, and so fell as he reached it, tumbling down to the basement floor with a cry. His hand smacked painfully against the bottom stair, but he managed to keep a hold on the doorknob.

Clump, clump, clump. Milton heard Porifera's shoes descending the stairs, heading straight toward him.

Milton scrambled to his hands and knees and crawled into the basement, hoping not to topple any stacks of pumpkin butter. His

mind raced; this was as far as his plan had gone. Now he needed someplace to hide the doorknob until Chloe had had enough time to escape.

I hope you're running, he thought. *Please, Chloe—run!*

Where was Porifera? The footsteps on the stairs had stopped. The man could be anywhere.

"Aha!" Porifera's voice issued from the darkness a moment before an electric click. The bare lightbulb at the center of the basement glared into life, revealing Porifera standing with his hand on the string.

Milton looked up from the ground. Porifera's eyes darted to the doorknob in Milton's hand. He glanced up, at the knobless door at the top of the stairs, then let his slithery eyes resettle on Milton. He uncurled one hand and held it out.

"Hand over the knob," he said.

Milton shook his head. The drainpipe opening was directly behind Porifera.

Porifera leaned down and reached toward Milton.

"Give it!" he said.

Milton tried to crawl away, but Porifera grabbed him by the collar.

Footsteps creaked across the wood above them, unmistakably Chloe's tread. Milton looked up at the sound and his heart sank, lifeboats and all. Chloe had not taken the chance to escape. But Porifera would take the doorknob, take the Nasselrogt children back to Urchin House, and take away their childhood.

"It seems your sister is the more sensible of you two," said

Porifera, glancing up at the sounds of Chloe's clops.

There was no hope for the Nasselrogt children.

Unless . . .

Milton was a skeeball enthusiast. He eyed the opening of the bottomless drain six feet away, and hefted the weight of the doorknob in his hand. He only had a moment before Porifera's attention would be back on him, but a moment was all he needed.

Milton tossed the doorknob toward the drain.

Porifera's eyes widened.

The doorknob bounced across the dirt floor, rolled to the edge of the drainpipe, and came to a rest there, as if peeking over a precipice.

Milton's ears may never have wiggled again.

Porifera grinned, released Milton, and turned to pluck the doorknob from the floor.

Above them, Chloe screamed.

It was a piercing shriek, pure terror. Milton had never heard anybody make a noise like it. He and Porifera froze and stared upward.

The pumpkin butter jars shook at the scream's sound. Dust filtered down from the ceiling.

The doorknob tilted one final degree, then dropped into the hole.

But Milton did not notice the small victory. He was staring at the ceiling, eyes tracing the sounds of his sister's frantic footsteps, running from something he couldn't see.

Milton and Porifera both winced at every scream. They heard glass shatter at one side of the house, and then the other. Chloe's footsteps ran back and forth. They heard furniture topple.

Milton sprang to his feet and scrambled up the basement stairs, Porifera on his heels.

"Chloe!" Milton shouted. He banged his fists against the door. "Chloe! Chloe!"

They heard her scream again, and her footsteps scrambling frantically up the stairs to the second floor. Milton, up against the door, could hear a sound like dozens of asthmatic puppies, their tiny little wheezes and gasps. He could hear a rasping, too, like somebody dragging branches over the floorboards.

Porifera tried to turn the spindle where the doorknob had been, but it was useless.

"Stand back!" he said, pushing Milton out of the way. Porifera stood on the top step, braced himself, and thrust his shoulder against the door. The door did not budge.

Chloe screamed again.

Porifera threw himself against the door again, and again.

"We're coming!" he shouted.

This child was his responsibility; Porifera would not allow anything to happen to her. Every scream stabbed at him like an accusing finger. He looked at Milton. The boy was frantic.

Porifera braced himself, mustering his strength, focusing all the guilt he usually kept stored with the butterflies in his stomach, and moving it to his shoulder. He aimed for a point past the knobless door, centered his weight, and then threw himself against the door like a battering ram.

Porifera bounced off the door like a bug off a windshield. His feet lost their purchase and he tumbled downwards like a dropped doll, bouncing painfully off all twelve steps before collapsing in a heap at the bottom.

"Chloe," Milton said, more softly. Her screams had ended, but still he could hear the tiny grunts and wheezes, the sounds like tree bark scraping the floor.

An incredible stench was wafting from beneath the door. *Squampkins!* thought Milton, picturing the thick black goo that had issued from the cut stem of the gourd.

Milton ran down the basement stairs, leaped over Porifera's unconscious form, and raced to the drainage hole. Even knowing how hopelessly deep it was, he tried to reach the doorknob, lying with his shoulder to the ground and his hand stretching down into the empty pipe.

The sounds from above had stopped. A storm of silence rained down from the upper floors of the Argyle house.

Milton had thought nothing could be more terrible than Chloe's screams. But the silence was worse by far.

Milton ran to the pile of tools in the corner of the basement, and grabbed a shovel and a hammer. He knocked one and then the other against the door at the top of the stairs, until his arms were

burning and numb with exhaustion. He splintered and dented the surface of the heavy door, but still it would not budge.

Some hours before dawn, Milton dropped the shovel and hammer, exhausted. He leaned against the door and let his heavy eyes close. He dreamt that he was starving, and standing before an enormous pit of candy in which he somehow knew were hiding the hands of the dead, waiting to pull him down into the earth.

The door opened, and Milton woke just in time to feel his face smack against the wood of the living room floor.

He rolled over and opened his bleary eyes to see Mr. Helsabeck towering over him.

"Eek," said Milton. Then the rest of the night before flooded his waking mind. "Where's Chloe?" he asked.

"Was that your sister's name?" Helsabeck asked. His voice sounded like his batteries were dying.

"What did you do to her?" Milton asked, crab-walking out from beneath Helsabeck until he could get to his feet.

Porifera groaned from the bottom of the stairs. Helsabeck ignored Milton's question and descended into the basement.

"Chloe!" Milton shouted. He looked around the morning-lit living room. Two of the windows had been shattered and broken glass dragged across the room. Some of the glass was rimmed in black goo. A lamp and a chest of drawers had been overturned. Books and papers were scattered and torn. The terrible stench of cut squampkin lingered, as if a soured buttermilk zombie was hiding beneath the sofa. "Chloe!"

There was no sign of her.

Porifera emerged from the basement, holding his head and squinting in the morning light.

"Where's Chloe?" Milton asked.

"Your sister's gone," said Helsabeck.

"What did you do with Chloe?" Milton was ready to throw himself at Helsabeck, even if the man did have a fondness for axes.

Helsabeck shook his head.

"Where is she?" Milton asked again.

"Maybe I'll find her when I find my Benny. This house . . ." Helsabeck said, his voice dripping with hopeless fatigue, "This house ate my son. This house eats children. And now it's eaten your sister. Those things in the yard . . ."

"What are you talking about?" Porifera said.

"The squampkins. The Nasstuhl Road Patch," said Helsabeck.

"*Nasal Rod*," said Milton. "We have to get Chloe back. Where is she?"

"She's gone." said Helsabeck.

"We're getting her back," said Porifera. Milton looked at him, surprised by the conviction in his voice.

Helsabeck just shook his head.

"What's going on here?" asked Porifera.

Helsabeck sighed. "Nothing good. I can only tell you what I know."

Helsabeck started walking through the wrecked living room and toward the open front door.

"Let's go to my house," he said. Milton and Porifera followed Helsabeck outside and onto the porch.

"The squampkins are gone." Milton froze on the worn boards of the porch.

All of the squampkins had vanished, the brown expanse of the dimpled and furrowed field filled with nothing but the thick, woody vines, coiling like sea serpents.

Milton looked at the hill, similarly barren beneath the great box elder.

Helsabeck did not stop, but continued quickly in a long arc that took him around the squampkinless patch and toward his own house across the street.

"What's going on here?" Porifera asked again.

"We're getting Chloe back," said Milton. "That's all I know."

"Good," said Porifera.

They hurried to catch up with Helsabeck, who had stopped to let the screeching school bus rumble slowly past him.

Beulah, the Milkhammers, and a busload of other kids nursing candy hangovers stared out.

After it passed, Milton followed the adults into Helsabeck's avocado-green house.

Chapter 23

The Things on the Other Side

Milton's Halloween evening had been bad, but Chloe's was worse. What Milton had mistaken for hopelessness was dread. Exactly how, Chloe did not know, but she felt certain that the Argyle house was potentially more terrible than the Urchin House zipper factory could ever be.

All night long she had been trying to piece together the story.

Mr. Helsabeck had a son named Benny, and they lived in the avo-cado house across the street from Charlie Argyle's. Argyle hated Benny Helsabeck. Argyle planted a squampkin patch that he was certain was going to make him rich on Halloween night. A man named Gardner Gray said, "What you sow, they will reap." Benny Helsabeck vanished on Halloween night, after all of the squampkins had been dragged across the street and into his front yard. Weeks later, Charlie Argyle vanished too.

Benny Helsabeck had vanished a year ago to the day that Chloe found herself in the Argyle house, listening to the squampkin patch waking outside, as Milton and Porifera headed toward the basement.

She was confused and frightened, and growing more so with each passing moment. She could not help but think back to a time when her biggest complaint had been the boredom of life under the care and protection of her mom and dad. She could not stop the tears from rolling down her cheeks.

Milton was saying, "We're going into the basement, Chloe. Hang *loose*, we can *handle* it."

Chloe wondered how he could refuse to hear the noises coming from the squampkin patch, burbling around the house from all sides. Hundreds of soft crunching and squilching sounds, somewhere between an egg hatching and a bony, juicy frog being crushed underfoot.

Chloe looked at Milton and swallowed the lump in her throat. She began to say *don't go*, but Milton had already stepped through the basement door and slammed it behind him.

"Run, Chloe, run, run!" he shouted from beyond the door.

She took a step toward the front door. Maybe she could get out. Maybe she could get past whatever was happening in the squampkin patch.

Something clawed frantically at the door, like a puppy trying to get in. Chloe froze.

There was a *pop* as the lightbulb outside broke, casting the porch into darkness.

Another pair of claws joined the first against the bottom of the door. Then more. Chloe backed away.

There was a tapping on the glass of the front window. The

sound of movement outside the house suddenly swelled, a sliding and crunching that swarmed in as if an army of heavy-tailed rodents were sweeping through the grass and across the porch.

Claws clicked against the glass of the windows. The rasping scramble against the front door grew more frantic, and then began to climb.

"Run! Run, Chloe!" Milton's shout was muffled by the heavy basement door.

Where could she run to? She caught a glimpse of something orange, the size of a cat's paw, flit past a window. But when she turned to look, she found only her own reflection in the glass.

She felt desperately alone in the house, and terribly frightened. The tears were now flowing freely down her cheeks.

The scrabbling at the front door inched higher, the unseen claws reaching for the doorknob.

Chloe ran forward as the knob turned and the door began to swing inward.

It opened an inch before she threw herself against it, slamming it closed and knocking over whatever was pushing from the other side. She heard angry hisses, then pattering thumps like a basket of cantaloupes overturning onto the porch.

Chloe's fingers fumbled at the doorknob, trying to lock it, but it twisted back and forth violently in her grasp, the things on the other side eager to get in.

The door pushed in against her. Chloe gasped.

A hand the size of a baby's, three-fingered, orange-skinned, and

black-palmed, reached through the gap and clutched at her pant leg.

Chloe jerked her leg away and threw herself against the door, shutting it on the tiny orange arm. Its owner hissed angrily on the far side. Another orange arm reached in above the first. Chloe's hand left the doorknob and reached for the security chain on the doorjamb.

She frantically slid the chain from its track on the door and fell back.

The door jerked inward, pulling the chain tight and leaving a three-inch gap between jamb and door. A half-dozen orange-skinned hands were thrust through the gap, all of them trying to divine Chloe's location. The babyish hands clenched and opened, again and again, hungry to dig their fingers into her.

Chloe backed away, her eyes focused on the tiny, shiny finger-nails, black like beetle backs. She did not notice the sound of small hands smacking against the front window until her attention was drawn by the brittle cracking of glass.

A dozen orange figures could be seen dimly through the window's reflection of the room, madly flailing at the glass. Chloe's eyes had only just begun to distinguish the figures outside when the glass shattered, and they tumbled into the living room in a shower of glass.

Chloe screamed.

They were squampkins.

They were humanoid, stalking upright on stubby little legs, backs bent, heads wrinkled like a turtle's. Their skins were the same burning orange of their gourd-form rinds, veined with green. Dark splotches marked their bellies and the pits of their eyes. Vines extended from the bases of their spines like tails, each one leading back to the soil beneath the patch that until recently had borne Chloe and Milton's family name.

The squampkins' eyes were no more than dimples in the thick rind-flesh of their faces. Their mouths were frog-lipped slits that gaped hungrily as they hissed, stringy mucous like the guts of a pumpkin stretching from top to bottom.

They rolled toward Chloe like spilled water, hissing and panting, arms outstretched, little fingers hungrily grasping.

Chloe screamed again and broke into motion. She ran to the kitchen, her feet hitting the dark linoleum just as the back door swung open. Another legion of squampkins, their spinal vines stretching up the hill to the box elder behind the house, swarmed in from the porch. Chloe stopped short, then ran back the way she had come.

A dozen squampkins had wriggled in through the gap at the front door, thirty more through the front window, and the same number from the now-broken side window.

A lamp crashed to the floor, and then another, darkness spreading suddenly throughout the living room.

The first squampkin reached her, its tiny hands digging into the fabric of one pant cuff and holding fast. Another grabbed her shoe.

Chloe screeched and kicked the creature away from her. She could feel the tiny fingers scratching at her shin through her pants.

A third threw itself at her legs, clinging to her other shin.

The creatures were pouring in from all sides. There were too many; she could not escape.

The vines, Chloe thought. *They're still attached to their vines.*

A dozen squampkins were threading their way between the legs of the table by the side window. Just before they reached her, Chloe dodged right and ran in a circle around the table. The squampkins followed, vines coiling behind them, gaining.

Chloe leaped over the vines where they led in through the window and ran for the stairs.

The squampkins that had followed her circuit around the table lurched forward and stopped, their spinal vines looped around the table legs. They were caught.

A victory, but a small one: Dozens more of the creatures were in the house, waddling swiftly after Chloe. They threw themselves onto her legs, climbing madly, as if hoping to find Faye Wray in Chloe's ear.

She clawed at them and threw them off, prying away their strong little fingers.

Chloe reached the stairs and scrambled upward, screaming as a squampkin wound its hands into her hair. She shook her head, slamming the creature into the railing. It let go and tumbled down the stairs.

Reaching the second floor, Chloe dove into Charlie Argyle's bedroom, four squampkins still clinging to her legs and back. At least sixty more were tumbling over each other in their scramble up the stairs after her. Dozens of vines snaked through the open windows, the front door, and the kitchen.

Chloe grabbed the bedroom door and slammed it closed on the vines trailing behind her four attackers. The creatures hissed in pain, two of them dropping to the floor.

Chloe slammed the door again, and again. The two remaining squampkins tumbled off, hissing angrily and clutching at their stems. All four creatures retreated toward the open doorway and Chloe kicked them out, locking the door behind them.

The squampkins' tiny fingernails immediately began scrabbling against the wood.

Chloe backed into the center of the room and tried to collect herself. She had shut the squampkins out, but how long would it last? She had nothing to use as a weapon, and there were more creatures than she could possibly face alone.

Thump. A dull thud sounded through the ceiling above Chloe. *Thump, thump.*

The squampkins were on the roof.

Other than the door, the only way out of Argyle's bedroom was the window. Chloe ran to it and looked outside.

At the top of the hill, Chloe could see dozens of squampkin vines rising like swami-charmed ropes into the great box elder tree.

Suspended from its branches, the vines seemed to drift toward Chloe's place at Argyle's window, waver for a moment, then land with a *thump* on the roof above.

The squampkins were dropping from the branches of the mighty tree and down onto the Argyle house.

Chloe had been wrong about the window. It was not the only other way out of the room. It was another way in.

Outside Charlie Argyle's bedroom, dozens of squampkins piled against the door, raking their beetle-black fingernails against the wood, hissing and mewling their greed.

The door muffled the sound of glass breaking inside the bedroom, and Chloe's final scream.

Fainter still was the sound of Milton calling to his sister from the basement below.

All at once, the squampkins stopped scratching at the door to Argyle's bedroom. They turned and crawled down the stairs, following their own snaking vines back the way they had come— out through the windows, the front door, and the kitchen, to the patch.

The squampkins were satisfied. The reaping was done.

Chapter 24

The Pumpkin/Chocolate Trials, October 12–31

The morning after Halloween, Milton found himself sitting on a sofa next to Porifera in the avocado house of James Helsabeck. Milton remembered that his father used to sit him down on the sofa like this for "important talks," but he could not remember what any of those many talks had been about.

In the shock of Chloe's disappearance, Milton's brain was a fuzz of meaningless noise.

Helsabeck returned to the room with three mugs of coffee and a stack of torn pages wedged in his armpit.

"My milk is chunky," yawned Helsabeck, "so I brought you coffee. I hope you don't mind."

"Do you have sugar?" Milton asked.

Helsabeck nodded wearily, gesturing to a clown-shaped bowl on the coffee table as he put a mug of coffee in front of each of them.

"So what's going on?" asked Porifera. "Where's Chloe Nasselrogt?"

Helsabeck shook his head, then tossed the stack of paper onto the table.

"It's time for my morning nap. There might be an explanation in there." Helsabeck collapsed into a wingback chair and curled up like a potato bug.

Milton recognized the sheets of paper: They were the missing pages from Charlie Argyle's "Pumpkin/Chocolate Trials."

"What is this?" Porifera asked, lifting the pages.

Milton poured his mug of coffee into the sugar bowl, swirled the sludge to mix it, and took a sip.

"Maybe it's how we find Chloe," he said, taking the pages from Porifera and beginning to read. The first page was ripped, and it began

> . . . er 12
>
> A familiar bald head and gold teeth on the front porch this morning. Gardner Gray. Smiling at me like I had just stepped in a dog's business. Told me that my squampkin patch was a "thing of terrible beauty."
>
> He told me the patch needs "an appetizer." Talks about the squampkins like they're more animal than plant. If Gardner Gray is not crazy, the world is not sane. But if what he says works. . . .
>
> The night after tomorrow, the night of the

last full moon before Halloween, I'm supposed
to "sow" the patch. Whatever I scatter among the
vines, says Gray, the squampkins will gather on
Halloween night. If I scatter money, I'll wake up
on November first a rich man.

They take their booty underground. I'll only
need to wait a few weeks for the squampkins to
wither. Then shovel my way to buried treasure.

When I asked how squampkins could gather
anything, Gray said, "With their hands." Acted
like my question had been a foolish one.

When I asked him if anybody could get hurt,
he said, "Quite possibly. But only if you get in
their way. They're not killers, only collectors. But
oh yes, quite possibly." The man smiles at the
strangest times.

The words "They're not killers, only collectors" had been circled
in red pencil. There was a red pencil lying on the coffee table; Milton realized that Helsabeck had done the circling.

I saw his truck when he was leaving. Painted
red like a cartoon brick. Maybe you'd call it scarlet. Before he left, we both heard footsteps in
the kitchen. I thought it was my intruder, back

again, but Gardner Gray laughed at me. He said
that they usually sleep during the day, but with a
squampkin patch as healthy as mine, I was liable
to hear all sorts of strange things.

Milton skipped through a few pages of recipes and sketches.
Then:

October 13
    The moon is full, as heavy in the sky as I've ever
seen. If Gray is leading me wrong, I threw away
nearly three thousand dollars tonight. I spent all
afternoon shredding ten- and twenty-dollar bills
and crumpling them into tight little balls.
    I waited until the moon was high in the sky. I
swear I heard movement in the squampkin patch,
but when I looked, saw nothing out of the ordi-
nary.
    Half an hour ago, I went out and scattered the
silver dollars and crumpled-up bills among the
vines.
    Eighteen days until Halloween. For my patis-
serie's sake, I hope this works.

October 24
    James Helsabeck came calling at the shop to-

day. Asked me to spend less time with his son. I thought it was some kind of a joke—I hadn't seen Benny in weeks. And was all the more cheerful for it.

But then he says Benny's been crossing the street to my house daily. Benny told him that he was helping me with the shop.

I was stymied until it hit me. Benny was my intruder! Of course! It only makes sense, the little sneak is violating my house and stealing my candy!

Could barely maintain my composure in front of James. Told him to call me next time Benny was coming over, and I'd be sure to send him home.

October 25

It worked! James telephoned me, said Benny was on his way over.

I was waiting at the back door with a bucket of sourdough slop. Benny barely got a foot on the back step before I jumped out and doused him in fetid stink.

He ran home. Hopefully he won't be back.

And he was crying to beat the band. Icing on the cake.

Milton handed the next few pages to Porifera, who was shaking his head as he read, trying to keep up.

October 28

Envelope in the mail from M & R Ake, Inc. today. The letter was from Gardner Gray. He says he'll need his commission, for instructing me on sowing the patch.

He's going to stop by on November 13. He'll want 10 percent of the money I get from the squampkin patch. The letter sounded threatening. Said if I don't have the money, he might have to invite me into his delivery truck. What does that mean?

October 30

This time of year always reminds me of the Philistines who surround me. Nobody appreciates my art. I watch parents buy buckets of the cheapest, most gaudily wrapped candy they can get. My sweetshop is ignored, shelves of candy forsaken.

The children are giddy, bouncing around town, screeching about Halloween. Disgusting.

But maybe tomorrow night is my ticket out of this child-infested town. If what Gardner Gray says is true, tomorrow night will make me a rich man.

Where would the squampkins get my money? Would they hurt anybody to get it? Gardner Gray said they were collectors, not killers. But still . . . I try not to think about it.

I flip through earlier pages of this journal, and remember the pumpkin chocolate-chip cookies that inspired it. How far from away I've come. How perfect would those cookies have been for Halloween?

Maybe I'll bake a batch, for the sake of the holiday.

October 31

I am distracted by anticipation. Waiting for night to come. For the squampkins to act.

I'm excited. Ate three dozen pumpkin chocolate-chip cookies on my own. I must be nervous.

Milton turned to the next page, and found mad scribbles scrawled across it in frantic, ragged loops.

THEY'RE ALIVE! The squampkins! Like little . . .

Then, further down the page:

> . . . in my shop. COLLECTING CANDY! I
> tried to stop them, they overwhelmed me, like a
> wave of hideous children. I'm covered in bruises.
> Frantic. Can't call the police. No phone number
> for M & R Ake or Gray. The candy's gone. They've
> cleared the shop. Only my personal stash remains.
> THEY'RE TAKING THE CANDY UNDER-
> GROUND. What in the name of . . .

Scrawled into the margin, Charlie had written:

> CAUGHT ONE! It's in the freezer! I trapped
> it inside and cut the vine. THE STENCH!!

Milton remembered the dark, child-shaped smudge he had
seen in Argyle's freezer. His eyes darted down to the bottom of the
page:

> The squampkins, those THINGS, they're
> crossing the street. Maybe the Helsabec . . .

The bottom of the *c* formed a ragged trench across the paper, nearly pushing through it. It was the final page, the end of the "Pumpkin/Chocolate Trials," and the end of Argyle's story.

Milton handed the sheet to Porifera, who snatched it up and squinted at the narrative's end with equal parts confusion and disbelief. The treadmill that powered Milton's brain was running at about six hamster-power, not nearly enough to piece together what he had just read with what Chloe had told him about the "Pumpkin/Chocolate Trials." Milton took a sip of coffee-tinted sugar sludge from the clown bowl and felt another eight hamsters get on the wheel.

"What is this?" asked Porifera, putting down the final page.

"That," said Helsabeck, eyes still closed, "is how I lost my son, a year and a day ago."

"I don't understand," said Porifera.

"Nobody understands. Nobody thinks I'll find him," said Helsabeck. "Nobody believes me—not the police, not the private detectives who take my money and then laugh at my story. They ask me if the little orange men took my son to the chocolate factory. What does that mean?"

Milton could spot an Oompa Loompa reference from a mile off, but silently sipped his coffee-sugar as Helsabeck continued.

"Maybe they meant something about Argyle's chocolates. I know that's why Benny was hanging around him. Although . . . about three weeks before Halloween last year he stopped eating the chocolates. He was hoarding them—had a pillowcase full of

chocolates in his room. Strangest thing. And then, a few days later, I caught him sneaking back into the house in the dead of night with the pillowcase empty. I remember the moon was full; it was so bright that night. Strangest thing . . ."

Helsabeck lapsed into a few moments' silence.

"I thought if I watched closely enough this year I could piece it together." The lids of Helsabeck's bloodshot eyes dragged open slowly. One could believe that no matter how much time the man spent with his eyelids shut, he never slept. "And then, when I saw that the squampkins were growing again, were coming back, I thought I could stop them. Chop up the vines. But they slithered around my ankles, they . . . I was scared. Just like I was scared when they took Benny."

Helsabeck nearly needed pliers to wrench those last words from his throat, and the effort left him silent.

"Do you understand any of this?" Porifera asked, turning to Milton.

"Not yet, but . . ." said Milton. "Wait! I'll get the rest of the 'Pumpkin/Chocolate Trials'!"

He desperately needed to move, so full was he of sugar and coffee. He leaped to his feet and sprinted out of the avocado house, returning moments later with Charlie Argyle's journal, which he threw on the coffee table between Porifera and Helsabeck.

Milton took a deep breath, and an even deeper swig of coffee sugar. About three dozen hamsters were on the wheels. Maybe if he talked through the story aloud he could piece it together. Milton inhaled as if he were going to inflate a zeppelin, then began.

"A man named Charlie Argyle used to live across the street, in the house me and Chloe decided to move into when we came here. Argyle's sweetshop is right there on the corner, across the yard from his house. He made cakes and cookies and pastries and pies and unbelievably wonderful candies." Milton paused to wipe the drool from his lip and the tear from his eye.

"But he hated children, especially Mr. Helsabeck's son, Benny. Argyle wanted to move his bakery to someplace where adults buy pastries and candy, like Paris. But there was no way he could get together enough money for that—until he started trying to find the perfect winter gourd for his pumpkin chocolate-chip cookies. His search put him in contact with the Winter Squash Underground, who put him in contact with M & R Ake, Inc. and a bald-headed, gold-toothed man named Gardner Gray. They gave him the squampkin seeds."

Milton paused to flip forward through the journal, his eyes dancing over the page. He took another sip of coffee-sugar. Hamsters started having heart attacks, but others took up the slack.

"He planted the squampkin seeds and pretty soon the things had taken over his whole patch. Gardner Gray told him they would make him rich, and promised to come back later and explain to him how. Around this time, Benny had started sneaking into Argyle's house to steal candy."

A vital piece of the story suddenly fell into place for Milton. His eyes flashed. "Good hamsters!" he exclaimed.

Porifera and Helsabeck looked at him. "Never mind that hamster part," Milton said. "Here's what's important: Benny was sneaking into Argyle's house to steal candy. So he was in the house when Gardner Gray came to tell Argyle how to sow the squampkin patch. See? See?"

Porifera and Helsabeck shook their heads. Milton tried to take another sip of coffee-sugar but Porifera stopped his arm.

"Slow down," said Porifera. "What do you mean, 'sow the squampkin patch'?"

"On the last full moon before Halloween, you're supposed to scatter whatever you most want over the squampkin patch. The squampkins develop a taste for it, and on Halloween night they come alive and collect. Argyle wanted money for his pastry shop in Paris, so he was going to scatter money over the patch.

"But Benny overheard Gray telling Argyle how the squampkins work. So on the night of the last full moon before Halloween, Benny got to the squampkin patch first.

"And Benny wanted candy. So he scattered candy over the squampkins. By the time Argyle got there with his money, it was too late. The squampkins already had a taste for candy."

Milton's eyes bounced between Helsabeck and Porifera, waiting for them to catch up. Porifera looked like his head was about to burst.

"And these squampkins are the things that took Chloe?" asked Porifera.

"I . . . think so," said Milton. "Why would they do that? Why did they take Benny?"

"It was Halloween," said Helsabeck. "Benny went trick-or-treating. He came back with two pillowcases filled with candy."

"Even though he was going to be getting more candy than he could ever eat from the squampkins?" asked Milton.

"More candy than my Benny could eat? There was no such thing," said Helsabeck.

"He sounds like a great boy," said Milton, reverently.

Helsabeck nodded. "By nightfall, Benny had eaten both of those sacks of candy."

"So the squampkins . . . they wanted to collect all the candy their vines could reach," said Milton.

"And Benny was full of candy," said Helsabeck. A tear fell down his cheek.

"The journal says they're not killers, just collectors," Milton said. "Maybe Benny's still underground. . . ."

The three of them sat for a moment, staring into space.

"So why Chloe?" wondered Milton. Run, hamsters, run, he thought. He took another sip of coffee-sugar. He saw the tears running down Helsabeck's cheeks.

Chloe's tears.

"Chloe cried in the squampkin patch," Milton whispered.

Porifera and Helsabeck looked at him.

"On the last full moon before Halloween," Milton said, "Chloe cried in the squampkin patch."

Chapter 25

Match the Skeleton

When Chloe awoke, she was not certain that she had opened her eyes, so absolute was the tunnel's darkness.

She realized that she was in the type of nightmare that waking will not solve. The night before, the squampkins had pulled her through Charlie Argyle's bedroom window, lowered her by vines to the yard, and dragged her underground.

The tunnel floor was clay. It was cold and slick against her hands as she pushed herself into a sitting position.

Silence roared like the sea in an empty shell, offset by only a faint purring, like hundreds of distant cats.

Chloe wrapped her jacket more tightly around herself and heard something rattle, like wooden matches in a box.

The matches from Charlie Argyle's oven!

Chloe fumbled in her pocket and pulled them out. She carefully withdrew a match and struck it against the side of the box.

The tiny flame snapped and flared.

She was in a sea of orange gourds and tangled vines. Hundreds of squampkins were clustered around her, curled into their harmless-seeming gourd forms.

Chloe froze, her breath caught in her throat by fear.

The purring sound was coming from inside the squampkins' thick, orange rinds. The vines spooled beneath them coiled and flexed ever so slightly, as if they were breathing.

"Ah!" Chloe yelped as the match burnt her fingertips. She dropped it, her stinging fingers already fumbling at the box for another match as she was cast again into darkness.

She was on her feet as the second match sparked to life. Her head touched the tunnel ceiling, and a little dirt sifted onto her shoulders. Her heartbeat quickened: She was underground. She was buried alive. She tried to will herself to stay calm.

To her right, the tunnel widened; she could see roots dangling from the ceiling. To her left, the tunnel narrowed, shrinking into darkness.

She took a step to the right. The purring from the squampkins rose to an angry simmer. Their thick rinds quivered.

Chloe took another step. In the wide chamber ahead, the matchlight just revealed a pale shape, something white, heaped against the far wall. One more step . . .

The squampkins' rinds were segmented like a pumpkin's, each one resembling a closed fist. As Chloe extended her foot, a dozen of those fists began to open.

"Ouch!" she shouted, dropping the second match as its heat nipped at her fingers. The box rattled, and a moment later, a third match flared.

The squampkins surrounding Chloe were transforming. The ridges slowly separated, two becoming arms, two more becoming legs. The squampkins flopped over and stood up, heads uncurling from beneath their mucous-strung bellies.

Chloe's heart hammered against her ribs; the match shook in her hand. Dirt sifted from the ceiling onto her shoulders and head. She could feel the walls closing in on her, the tunnel constricting like a throat and squeezing the breath out of her, burying her with this legion of *things*.

Breathe, she told herself.

She took another step toward the tunnel chamber.

Tiny, toadlike mouths gaped and hissed all around her. The creatures' eyes flashed as they moved forward, their arms outstretched.

The third match went out.

Chloe, trying desperately to breathe, groped for another match. Her hands shaking, she struck the match against the side of the box three times before it caught flame.

A dozen squampkins were lined up in front of her, taking tiny, hissing breaths, blocking her way.

Their message was clear: *Stay put.*

The feeble light of the match wavered with each of Chloe's shakily exhaled breaths.

The match flame steadied, and Chloe's eyes focused on the jumbled white shape against the far wall. Her panicked breath was arrested, choked in the back of her throat. The chamber was a dead end, a circular room with dozens of enormous roots dangling from its ceiling.

The white shape against the far wall was a pile of bones.

It was a child's skeleton, surrounded by candy wrappers and moldering mounds of year-old chocolate.

Chloe dropped the match as it burnt her fingers, and she fell again into darkness.

Chapter 26

Fried in Not-Pleasant

They carried a pickax, a shovel, and Helsabeck's goo-stained ax, marching in a line across the yard to the squampkin patch. They looked for all the world like four of the dwarves had called in sick.

"So where do we dig?" Porifera asked.

"I'm trying to think," said Milton, looking slowly over the patch. Not even the squampkin's vines were visible. The furrowed rows of earth were randomly dimpled, as if a giant had pressed thumbprints into the soft ground. *That's where the squampkins dug under,* thought Milton.

Helsabeck's weary, bloodshot eyes could have belonged to a paranoid basset hound.

"This is hopeless," he said, nervously.

Porifera wished he could drop Helsabeck on an ice flow and push him out to sea. Children who had lost their parents were bad enough. It seemed that parents who had lost their children were insufferable.

Milton glanced up at the box elder tree, furrowed his brow, and then tilted his head. Yes, the tree was off-kilter. It had somehow acquired a tilt, leaning slightly in the direction of the Argyle house.

"We might as well give up," said Helsabeck. "Who could use a nap? I know I could."

"Shut up, you soggy nit!" said Porifera. "We're getting Chloe back, and you're helping. Milton, where do we dig?"

Milton wished desperately that Chloe was there. Her keen powers of perception would have made short work of the clues leading to the site of her own burial.

Then he saw it. "There!" he said, pointing at the largest dimple in the field, an indentation in the empty patch the size of a kitchen sink.

Porifera and Milton ran to it and began to dig. By the time Helsabeck trudged over, they had settled into an efficient rhythm, Milton loosening the earth with his pickax and Porifera shoveling it to the side.

Helsabeck stood and watched, leaning on his ax.

Within minutes, they had burrowed a foot into the patch and reached the first of the squampkin vines.

"Helsabeck," said Porifera. "Chop, chop."

"You want me to hurry? Hurry what?" Helsabeck said.

"Let's see that ax get happy," said Milton. He thought of the stinky black goo from the cut vines, and covered his nose with his hula-girl tie.

Helsabeck stepped forward and let the blade of the ax rest on

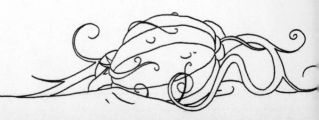

an exposed vine, establishing his aim. He drew back the ax, lifting it over his head. The squampkin vine twitched.

Helsabeck screeched like a school bus with bad brakes, dropped the ax, and sprinted across the street and into his house.

"What happened?" asked Porifera.

"The vine moved," said Milton.

Porifera shook his head and picked up the ax. It felt unnatural in his hands, and it took him four swings to get through the vine. By the time he did, both ends of the vine were spurting black goo as if Porifera had struck oil (oil that a long-dead, leprous tuna fish had been fried in).

"Not pleasant," he said, dropping the ax and covering his nose.

They tried to keep digging, but the smell was enough to make them gag. Milton went inside and rummaged through Argyle's kitchen until he found the vanilla extract. They soaked handkerchiefs and tied them across their mouths and noses. Long-dead, leprous, deep-fat-fried tuna fish infused with vanilla was not as offensive a stench, and they got back to digging.

The black goo gummed the earth and made it heavy; their progress slowed. Milton's pickax and Porifera's shovel stuck in the sludge, which did its best to wrestle the tools from the diggers' hands.

By lunchtime, Milton and Porifera's hands were blistered, their backs ached, and they were plastered with sticky, malodorous muck.

They collapsed by the side of the hole, panting.

"How much farther can it be?" said Milton.

"The only way we'll find out is digging," said Porifera. "I hope we get down there before nightfall."

"We can't let Chloe spend the night down there," Milton said, adding after a moment, "So what happens when we get her back?"

"Hmm?" Porifera tried to act like the question held little importance.

"Are you still going to try to take us back to Urchin House?"

"It's the best thing for you," Porifera said without thought.

"We hate it there," said Milton. "We don't belong in a zipper factory."

"Kids need work," Porifera said, wearily pushing himself to his feet. "You can lie around and think when you get older. Now let's get back at this hole."

Porifera groaned as he picked up the shovel. Milton, getting to his feet, saw Helsabeck approaching from across the street.

Helsabeck had brought a plate of peanut-butter-and-marshmallow sandwiches, along with embarrassed apologies for his cowardice.

"It's just like I was a year ago," he said. "Too frightened to act."

"These sandwiches are excellent," Milton said.

"They were Benny's favorite," said Helsabeck.

Milton saw Porifera scraping the marshmallows off of his

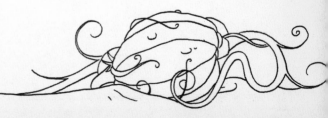

sandwich and intercepted, adding them to his own. As Milton ate two sandwiches and Porifera ate three, Helsabeck gave himself a peanut-butter mustache to counteract the squampkin-goo stench, and began chopping at the hole.

Working together, the three of them had dug down another foot and a half by midafternoon. The tangle of vines was getting thicker.

Milton heard a terrified screech, and assumed at first that Helsabeck had been frightened by an earthworm or a low-flying airplane. But as the screeching slowed to a stop, Milton glanced over his shoulder and saw that it was Beulah's school bus, from which the Milkhammer twins were descending.

"Beulah!" said Milton.

Porifera's shovel and Helsabeck's ax paused.

"She's a coal miner's daughter!" Milton said.

"Ooh. Does she know any songs?" Porifera asked.

"Yes! But that's not important right now! She knows how to dig!" Milton scrambled out of the hole and ran toward the bus. Several of the children onboard mistook his goo-and-mud-encrusted form for that of a young yeti, and screamed accordingly.

The screams got Brad and Erica's attention, but Beulah paid no mind, driving away.

"Beulah! Beulah!" Breathless, Milton reached the twins just as the bus rounded the bend and disappeared.

"You look terrible," one twin said, just as the other one said,

"You smell terrible." Both stepped back, covering their noses.

"Unholy mackerel," said Milton, "couldn't just one thing be easy?"

"The squampkins are gone," said a Milkhammer, almost at a whisper.

Milton nodded. "They took Chloe. They took her underground."

The Milkhammers were, for once, speechless. Milton had a sudden realization.

"That's what you were afraid of, that night in the squampkin patch," he said. "Not Helsabeck and his ax, but the squampkins. You saw them move."

The Milkhammers nodded.

"We didn't want to end up like Benny," said a Milkhammer.

"Or his dad. Everybody thinks he's sad and crazy because he said a pumpkin patch took his son," said the other.

"Sad and crazy isn't so far off the mark," said Milton. "I need Beulah's help. We're digging down to rescue Chloe."

"Who's this?" asked a filthy, smelly Porifera as he approached. He did not like the look of these kids; they had the arrogant swagger of the parented.

"Brad and Erica Milkhammer," said Milton, "this is Mr. Porifera. He's a villain, but he's also helping me rescue Chloe. It's kind of complicated."

"How do you do," said a Milkhammer.

"You smell even worse than Milton does," said the other.

"Hello, Brad." Porifera nodded to the leftward Milkhammer, then to the right. "Hello, Erica."

Milton's gast was flabbered. "You can tell them apart?"

"Sure," Porifera said. "I'm assuming Brad is the boy and Erica the girl."

"But they look exactly alike," said Milton, master of tact, then realized he needed to get back on track. "What about Beulah? Do you know how we can find her?"

"No," said Brad.

"Sure we do," said Erica. "I mowed her lawn this summer—I know where she lives."

"Great! Can you get her? Beulah's father was a coal miner. She could help us dig down to rescue Chloe. . . ."

"Brad! Erica!" Margery Milkhammer stormed over her front step. "What did I tell you about talking to yeti?!"

"Give us a few minutes—we'll sneak out!" said Erica, moments before Margery grabbed the twins' arms and dragged them across the lawn and into the house.

Mucky, malodorous Milton and Porifera watched the three Milkhammers vanish behind a slammed door.

"Let's get back to that hole," said Porifera.

The sun blushed as if embarrassed to meet the horizon, as Milton's pickax punched through the clay. A breeze whistled up through the small hole. They had reached the tunnel.

Yet there still remained a thick, final layer of squampkin vines blocking their entrance.

"We're almost there!" said Milton, dropping down and shouting into the hole, "Chloe! Chloe, can you hear me?"

He turned his ear to the hole, but he could hear no response.

"Stand back and let the ax work," said Porifera.

"Hang on, Chloe!" Milton shouted into the hole, as he climbed out of the way.

Helsabeck wrenched his attention away from the quickly setting sun and, swallowing his fear, began to chop at the vines.

Chapter 27

Hide Puckering

In the absolute darkness underground, Chloe could hear nothing but her own ragged breaths and the roar of panic in her head. The matchbox shook in her hand, rattling faintly; there were only two matches left.

Suddenly, a squampkin began to screech in pain. The sound drilled into Chloe's ears like ice picks.

Her fingers fumbled at the matchbox. The creature's screeching continued, an urgent rustling all around her, moving closer.

Her hands shook so badly that one of the matches spilled from the box and was lost at her feet. The match in her trembling fingers was the last, but she had to see. The unfixed horror of her imagination was too terrible to bear.

The tunnel leaped into view. In the orange, wavering light of the tiny flame, Chloe saw the screeching squampkin, its hands clutching the vine that wound from the base of its spine to the patch above and the ax blade severing it from the earth. Its head thrashed back and forth as it withered and emptied, deflating like a balloon, its thick hide puckering.

The squampkin's scream died with it. Chloe watched it collapse and darken, rotting before her eyes. All around her, the hundreds of other squampkins, still curled into gourds, rolled toward Chloe. The walls themselves, woven with vines, seemed to press closer.

Chloe felt as if the air were being sucked out of her.

She did not scream when the match burnt her fingers and flickered out. If she let herself scream, Chloe knew she would not be able to stop.

Chapter 28

Pants-Clad Plant

Helsabeck used his sleeve to wipe the sweat and squampkin goo from his brow, careful to leave his peanut-butter-moustache anti-stench barrier in place.

Milton stepped forward and lowered himself gingerly into the hole. As he raised the pickax above his head, he thought vaguely of something his mother had once told him about not sitting on the branch you were sawing. Unfortunately, the thought did not have time to complete itself before Milton had let the pickax fall, breaking through the tunnel roof on which he was standing.

He yelped as the clay crumbled beneath his feet. The rim of the hole flew past his head, and he was swallowed in darkness.

"Oof," he said, pushing himself up from the tunnel floor. The pickax had thunked into the clay just beside him, the sharp tip landing inches from Milton's hand.

Milton peered into the darkness. He was at the tunnel's tallest point, the ceiling several feet beyond his reach. It looked something like a giant Chinese finger trap, so thoroughly were squampkin vines woven into the walls.

"He's dead—leave him!" shouted Helsabeck.

"I'm okay!" shouted Milton in rebuttal.

"Run!" shouted Helsabeck, backing away from the hole.

"Quiet, you ninny!" said Porifera before calling to Milton, "Can you see Chloe?"

"No, I can barely see anything." Milton rubbed the seat of his pants. "No squampkins, either. But a lot of vines."

Milton was on a slope at the lower end of the tunnel, where it branched beneath the squampkin patch between the house and the street. The uphill stretch of tunnel led back toward the great box elder tree overlooking the Argyle house.

Porifera looked at the sun, which had gotten over its shyness and was three quarters of the way nestled into the horizon. Helsabeck was dancing from foot to foot, eager to flee.

"We'll have to widen the hole before any adults can squeeze down there," said Porifera. "And we're going to need a flashlight and a rope."

"I've got those!" shouted Helsabeck, turning and running toward his house. He nearly trampled Brad and Erica Milkhammer, who were heading for Porifera.

"Hi, Mr. Helsabeck," they said in chorus, as the terrified, sleepy man sprinted into his avocado house.

"Brad! Erica!" said Porifera. "What took you so long?"

"Our mom," said a Milkhammer twin.

"Mothers . . ." said Porifera, shaking his head in disgust.

"What about Beulah?" Milton called from the tunnel.

"We're about to bike over there and get her," Erica Milkhammer said. "Does she need to bring anything?"

"Whatever mining tools she has," Porifera said, watching the sun sink lower. "And tell her to hurry. It'll be dark by the time she gets here."

Helsabeck emerged from his house with a flashlight.

Milton began to hear a faint purring sound fill the tunnel. It seemed to grow as the pink rays of the setting sun faded above.

"I think something's happening," he called out to Porifera, pulling the pickax from the ground and holding it ready. "Argyle's journal said the patch wakes up at night."

"Sit tight," Porifera responded. "We've got a flashlight. Soon as I widen the hole, I'll come down and join you."

Helsabeck arrived, panting, and handed over the flashlight to Porifera.

"I couldn't find a rope," Helsabeck said.

"Dang," said Porifera. Then he saw the garden hose at the edge of the patch. "Grab that hose—we'll use it instead."

Milton watched the last painterly dawb of sunlight vanish from the rim of the hole above him. The purring swelled like an angry coffee pot.

"It sounds," Milton said softly, "like the squampkins are waking up." The purring, gurgling was all around. Vertigo suddenly swept over Milton. He had the sensation of sliding through the tunnel, and realized that the vines woven into the walls had all moved slightly.

"Get on your bikes and get us a Beulah," Porifera said to the Milkhammers. "We don't have time to spare."

The Milkhammers nodded and started toward their house.

Then the leftward twin paused and sniffed. Beneath the hideous stench of squampkin goo, the Milkhammer smelled something else. The twin's eyes settled on the peanut-butter smear beneath Helsabeck's nose and then went daffy, wandering in opposite directions.

Porifera had gotten on his belly beside the hole and now slid forward, handing the flashlight and one end of the hose down to Milton. He had pushed his entire right arm and head into the hole, as much of an adult as would fit through the small opening, when the sun slipped below the horizon.

The purring around Milton swelled dramatically, the vines coming to life like a pit of snakes.

Porifera yelled as the hole suddenly constricted around him like a puckering mouth.

Helsabeck jumped at Porifera's muffled cry, turning just in time to see the vines slithering into the hole, enwrapping the orphanmaster's other arm and swallowing him up to the belly. In a matter of moments, Porifera was trapped, his legs sticking out of the earth like some strange khaki-pants-clad plant.

Milton only vaguely understood what had happened, so suddenly had the tunnel vanished in pitch blackness. He heard the flashlight clatter onto the clay floor nearby and began fumbling toward the sound.

Helsabeck inhaled to scream, but before he could let out a peep he was interrupted by a giddy "Hehehehehehehehehehehe."

It sounded like a drunken squirrel trying to imitate a machine gun.

One of the Milkhammer twins was lying on the ground, eyes wandering in mad orbits, feet peddling, lips drawn back in a Cheshire grin, giggling uncontrollably.

Helsabeck kneeled over the child. "What's wrong? What's going on?" He was shaking so hard that a bit of peanut butter fell from his lip and splattered on the giddy twin's nose.

"Peanut butter!" shouted the other twin. "It's an allergic reaction!"

"Hehehehehehehehehehehehe!"

"The hospital! Mom!" The twin with a brain and spinal cord still cooperating ran across the patch toward the Milkhammer house.

Underground, Milton switched on the flashlight. Porifera squinted against the glare, raising his free hand to shield his eyes. The squampkin vines around his chest slithered and squirmed like a pot of boiling spaghetti. The end of the garden hose stuck out from between his armpit and the roiling vines.

"Urgh," said Porifera, his face turning bright red.

"They're awake!" said Milton. "The squampkins are awake!"

"Aagh!" Porifera screamed. Aboveground, Helsabeck was pulling on his foot. With each tug, the squampkin vines coiled tighter.

Margery Milkhammer, running across the squampkin patch, saw a pair of upside-down legs planted in the earth kick Helsabeck in the nose. He fell backward into the dirt.

"Hehehehehehehehehehehe," the Milkhammer twin behind him said.

"My baby!" cried Margery.

"It was my peanut-butter mustache," said Helsabeck, pointing at his upper lip.

"You poor, stupid, sad man!" cried Margery Milkhammer, as she scooped up her giggling child and ran to her car.

"Yes, I am all of those things," said Helsabeck.

Below him, dirt showered down on Porifera, falling into his ample nostrils. He snorted and squinted, then said to Milton, "I sent the Milkhammers to find that miner woman, Beulah. She'll dig you out. You need to find Chloe. Urgh."

"The vines are climbing down!" Milton said, pointing the flashlight at Porifera's chest. The squampkin vines were indeed following the crumbling dirt, snaking across Porifera's chest and shoulders, heading for his face.

"Find your sister," Porifera said.

Milton reached up and tried to take the inverted man's free hand, but the vines pulled Porifera's arm out of his reach.

"They're going to bury you!" Milton said.

Porifera gasped as the vines looped around his ears. He was being wrapped up like a mummy. A vine crawled over his mouth, and he jerked his head away. Porifera only had time to say one more thing before he was buried alive by the squampkin vines.

"Milton. Save Chloe. Your . . ." The vine slithered between his teeth. He snarled and bit down. The vine withdrew for just a moment, but it was long enough for Porifera to cry out, "Your parents are still alive!"

Then the vines poured downward and swallowed the orphanmaster entirely.

Chapter 29

Definitely in Trouble, Said the Hose

Porifera's legs were still, bent at the knee, the heels of his galoshes not quite touching the ground behind him.

Helsabeck sat slumped next to them, suddenly feeling just as alone and frightened as he had for most of the past year. He needed a marshmallow sandwich and a nap.

The garden hose was calling his name.

The hose lay coiled near Porifera's waist. "Helsabeck. Mr. Helsabeck," it said.

"Hello?" Helsabeck said, talking into the end of the hose.

"Helsabeck! It's Milton! The squampkin vines ate Porifera," said the hose.

"Oh," said Helsabeck. How often could a person be surprised by the worst possible turn of events?

"I'm going to find Chloe and then come back here. When the Milkhammers get back with Beulah, shout into the hose so I know."

"Um, one of the Milkhammers is down," said Helsabeck. "My

peanut-butter moustache attacked him. Her. Him. Her."

"Which one was it?"

"I don't know, I can't tell them apart."

"But only Erica knows where Beulah lives," said the hose.

"Oh. So we might be in trouble," said Helsabeck.

"No, we're *definitely* in trouble," said the hose. "We just might not have a way out of it now."

Underground, Milton could feel Helsabeck's pessimism trickling down through the garden hose. Or maybe that was drool.

"All right, whatever," said Milton. "We'll burn that bridge when we get to it. I'm going to find my sister."

He dropped the hose.

A postage stamp of yellow galosh rubber visible through the snarl of vines above was the only remaining evidence of Yon Kinsky Kozinsky Porifera. Milton touched his flashlight to his brow in wary salute, then turned toward the darkness.

"Chloe!" he shouted. "Chloe!"

There were four tunnels branching away from him downhill, and one steadily narrowing tunnel leading upward. Unless Chloe answered him, he could only guess which direction to go.

"Chloe!" he shouted again, and then waited.

There was no answer but the purr and gurgle of the squampkin tunnels. Wherever he shone the flashlight over the tunnel walls, the vines shirked back, tightening their weave and pelting the floor with loose soil.

"Chloe!" he shouted. All day Milton had been denying himself permission to think a certain thought. Now it came bubbling up in his mind like bathtub flatulence: *Maybe there was a reason Chloe was not answering him.*

Chapter 30

The Sea of Angry Winter

The pitch-black tunnel around Chloe constricted. The rustling and shifting, the tiny asthmatic breaths of the squampkins, were bearing in on her. Chloe's eyes, wide and blind, shone with tears. She pressed into the wall behind her and the squampkin vines woven there pressed back, eager to embrace her.

Horror built inside of her, roiling like storm clouds in her brain.

A distant sound reached Chloe through the maze of tunnels. It was familiar in tone: a voice. She strained to listen.

Chloe. It was her brother's voice, far away, echoing.

Milton was in the tunnels.

Embarrassed banshees the world over would tip their hats in respect, for, in one breath, a full day and a full night's worth of screams erupted from Chloe all at once.

Milton ran uphill, the flashlight's disk of illumination bobbing against the squirming walls of the vine-woven tunnel. The ceiling grew steadily lower, the walls narrower.

He took the left-hand path at the first branching of the tunnel, following the sound of Chloe's scream. He nearly had to crawl on his hands and knees through the narrow passage, holding the pick-ax awkwardly before him, the squirming squampkin vines rasping against his shoulders.

The scream faded. Milton tried to push the image of Porifera, swallowed alive by the squampkin vines, from his mind.

The network of tunnels was far larger than he ever would have imagined. He realized that they must extend beyond the borders of Argyle's yard.

"Chloe!" he shouted at the next branch of the tunnel.

"Milton!" Her voice came from the right.

Milton followed, the tunnel widening enough that he could stand and run.

"Milton!" Chloe sounded as if she were just behind him. He skidded to a stop on the slick clay floor and aimed the flashlight in the direction of her voice.

There was a vine-rimmed hole, like a window between tunnels, in the wall before him. It was as big around as a manhole cover and a little below Milton's eye level. He crouched and shone the flashlight through.

Against the far wall, in the glare of the flashlight's beam, he saw Chloe's tear-stained cheeks. She raised a hand to shield her eyes.

"Chloe!"

"Milton!"

"Hold on, I'll crawl through," said Milton, dropping the pickax through the window and getting a leg up on the rim.

"Wait . . ." said Chloe. But it was too late. Milton had already squirmed halfway through the opening by the time his flashlight bobbed downward to reveal the hundreds of squampkins carpeting the tunnel floor.

They scattered from the light, leaving the illuminated circle of floor bare, then turned to look at him. Just beyond the edges of the flashlight's beam, hundreds of pairs of tiny eyes gleamed in the darkness, staring at Milton.

He froze, one leg and one arm in the tunnel behind, his head, other leg and other arm in the Chloe-and-squampkin-filled tunnel ahead.

"Chloe," Milton whispered, "you're surrounded by squampkins."

I have said before that Chloe was the observant one. She nodded.

Milton felt the vines along the edge of the window scrape against his chest like stone-scaled serpents. He gasped. *The opening was squeezing shut around him.*

Milton grunted and scrabbled forward, trying to get his other arm through the opening so that he could pull himself through.

"No!" Chloe yelled.

The squampkins watched, hissing, a sound of anticipation.

Milton yelled as the vines pinched into his shoulder, forcing him to drop the flashlight, which clattered to the floor and cast a cone of light onto Chloe.

Chloe could not see Milton's struggle, only hear the grunts and gasps issuing from the darkness.

Milton yelped, and Chloe heard something splat wetly against the clay floor.

"Milton?"

Chloe could not help but wonder whether Milton, or half of Milton, had just landed on the tunnel floor.

"Milton?" she said again, softly.

All was darkness beyond the glare of the flashlight. The squampkins turned back to Chloe, resuming their watch. Hundreds of eyes and thousands of shiny black fingernails gleamed in the meager electric light.

"I'm okay." Milton's voice came out of the darkness a moment before the flashlight was lifted.

Chloe exhaled. The squampkins turned back toward her brother, hissing angrily. Milton hefted the pickax and looked at the sea of creatures between him and his sister.

"They're not doing anything," he said.

"They only get mad when I try to move."

Milton shone the light downward, sweeping it over the squampkins. They scattered away from the beam.

"They're afraid of the light," Chloe said.

"Right," said Milton. "Maybe I can clear you a path. When they move, walk toward me."

With the way behind him closed off, Milton had no idea which

way they would go, but at least they would be together.

He shone the light directly in front of Chloe, sending squampkins scurrying away. She stepped forward, triggering a chorus of angry hisses. Milton dragged the flashlight's beam slowly downward, clearing a path before her.

She took three steps before the squampkins surged forward, like water from a broken dam. A hundred of them swarmed into the light, their tiny fingers grasping Chloe's legs. A hundred more turned just as abruptly and swept toward Milton.

The screams of both Nasselrogt children filled the tunnel. Chloe was swept back and thrown against the wall by a multitude of tiny hands. Milton was knocked to the ground, the pickax and flashlight tumbling across the floor. His screams were quickly muffled as the squampkins piled on top of him.

Beneath layer upon layer of the angry creatures, Milton curled into a ball, feeling their hungry little hands trying to pry his own hands away from his face.

Chloe screamed. The flashlight showed only a teeming pile of squampkins, covering Milton entirely.

She crouched, grabbed an armful of squampkin vines, and yanked. Several of the creatures were pulled from the pile, but twice that number immediately took their places in the fray.

A sudden thought struck Chloe: *The squampkins were not interested in hurting Milton, only in keeping her in place.* At least she hoped so.

She turned and sprinted toward the chamber where the skel-

eton lay. Her theory proved true. She took only a few steps before
the sea of angry winter squash rolled off of Milton and swarmed
around Chloe.

As soon as her brother was free, she froze. The squampkins
came to a rest surrounding her, staring at her with their tiny black
eyes.

Milton pushed himself wearily to his feet.

"Are you okay?" she asked.

Milton nodded. "Let's not try that again."

"What do we do now?"

Brother and sister stood on either side of the squampkin pile.

"I'll need to find another way out," said Milton. "The way I
came in is blocked." He nodded toward the puckered opening that
had nearly cost him an arm and a leg.

"What's over there?" Milton shone his flashlight towards the
chamber beyond Chloe.

"A dead end. And a dead body," said Chloe.

"What?"

"A skeleton, surrounded by candy wrappers."

"Benny . . ." whispered Milton.

Chloe nodded. Milton turned and shone his flashlight down
the opposite length of tunnel.

"Nothing doing there," he said. The tunnel sloped downward away from him, narrowing as it went until it cut off entirely, like the inside of an ice cream cone.

"Don't . . . you won't leave me here, will you?" Chloe said.

Milton turned back and saw new panic in her eyes.

"I won't leave you," he said.

He took a step forward, and a hundred squampkins spun to hiss at him.

"Don't make them mad," Chloe said.

Milton put his hands up defensively.

"I just want to see . . ." He edged his way toward the open chamber beyond Chloe. Squampkins hissed and gurgled, eyes gleaming wickedly from the darkness as they followed Milton's progress.

"Don't get too close to me. They'll attack again," Chloe whispered.

The beam of his flashlight fell on Benny's bones. Milton stopped dead. The squampkins waited.

"Hello, Benny," Milton said.

"Well?" said Chloe.

"I think he's dead." Milton swept the beam across the chamber. The walls were all similarly woven with squampkin vines, impossible to dig through with a pickax alone. He directed the beam upward, and saw the ceiling heavy with enormous roots. The largest were the size of elephant trunks, and dangled far into the chamber.

Milton realized that the roots on Benny's side of the room were lower than those on the other, as if the tree above them were tilted at an angle.

The great box elder! thought Milton. It was the squampkins' tunnels that had undermined the root system, lending a perilous tilt to the enormous tree.

In the dark, it was impossible to see Milton's ears wiggling.

Chapter 31

Count Twiddles

Helsabeck sat in the moonlight next to Porifera's legs. He spent some time listening to the faint purring sound that came from the end of the garden hose, but grew frightened and decided to practice his thumb twiddling instead. Since Benny had vanished, he had whiled away many hours seeing how many twiddles he could count.

The night was otherwise silent.

But then, as Helsabeck was completing the seven hundred and forty-ninth levorotatory rotation of his left thumb around his right, there was the muffled *thunk* of metal hitting wood.

Helsabeck untwiddled his thumbs and looked at the ax lying at his side. He certainly did not seem to be chopping anything.

The sound came again, and again, from the top of the hill behind him. He used Porifera's left calf to pull himself to his feet, and looked up at the large, slightly tilted box elder, underneath which could clearly be heard the sound of chopping wood.

From beneath the box elder, Milton could see two large roots that seemed to anchor the entire tree and keep it from toppling over.

He propped the flashlight in the center of the chamber, walked to the nearest root, and began chopping at it. He could just barely reach the ceiling with the pickax's blade, but a day's practice had lent him no small skill at the tool's use, and he quickly chipped away at the wood.

From where she stood, cornered by the squampkins, Chloe could not see her brother's progress. The squampkins showed only a passing interest in the chopping sounds coming from the neighboring chamber. Their terrible attention remained focused on Chloe.

Chips of wood flew around Milton, the root giving way under the force of the pickax's blows. The first root was as big around as a fat man's thigh, and by the time he had chopped through it, Milton was breathing hard and sweating, despite the subterranean November chill.

"One more to go," he called out to Chloe. "How are you holding up?"

Chloe didn't answer.

"Chloe?" Milton called into the darkness.

". . . I'm okay," she said, unconvincingly.

The other root anchoring the tree was even larger. Trickles, then streams of loose dirt fell on Milton as he squared up to swing the pickax.

The last few months had trained Milton to anticipate the worst possible outcome of any action, and a terrible thought crept into his brain: *What if the tree, rather than falling over, fell down?* He could imagine the tons of heavy wood crashing into the earth like a piston, making chunky Milton chowder with Benny-bone croutons.

Milton shook the thought from his head and made ready to swing the pickax again. The second root, wider than Milton's middle, was pulled tight as a piano wire by the tree's weight.

He drew back the pickax, took a breath, and swung. The blade thunked deep into the wood. Milton exhaled, and pulled the pickax out.

The *snap* was so loud and so sudden that it knocked Milton to the ground, the pickax spinning out of his hand.

Chloe and the sea of squampkins turned their heads as one toward the sound.

Milton rolled onto his back and watched the pickax rotate in the air above his soft, exposed belly.

The enormous root holding the box elder upright had broken in half, each end curling back like a party favor. The tree groaned mightily, a waking giant, and earth began to shower down into the chamber.

Milton's eyes were focused on the gleaming end of the pickax, describing a slow rotation through space, end over end, as it spun toward him.

The whole tunnel shook around Chloe; heavy clods of dirt fell from the ceiling. A stone dislodged from between the woven squampkin vines struck her shoulder.

"Aye!" she cried out. At the sound, the squampkins' attention snapped back to her.

The box elder began to tilt, the shallow roots tearing out of the ground.

The pickax tumbled downward. Milton decided that one belly button was sufficient, and rolled on his side. The blade landed with a *thunk*, piercing Milton's suit and vest and digging into the clay beneath him.

Chloe covered her head as larger sections of the ceiling caved in on her, rocks and chunks of dirt raining down.

The squampkins swept forward, scrambling up the walls behind Chloe, their vines trailing. Within moments, they were all around and above her, holding fast to the walls, their vines blocking the tumbling debris from hitting her. She was safe. *The squampkins were protecting her.*

Milton looked up just in time to see the root structure of the box elder lift away from him, like a plastic lid peeled from a pot of icing, and reveal the moonlit sky above.

Helsabeck had the best view of all.

He watched the tree groan and shudder, tilting slowly at first as its roots pulled away from the earth. The shadow of the enormous tree loomed over the Argyle house.

The box elder finally admitted that it was no longer a tree, but lumber, and let go. It slammed like a thousand hammers into the Argyle house, demolishing the roof and smashing easily through

two floors before slamming down into the kitchen.

Wind and debris blew past Helsabeck, scattering the remnants of the house across the lawn.

Larger chunks of the house, furniture, and loosened lumber caromed across the patch. Sofa cushions cartwheeled through the front yard. Jars of pumpkin butter rolled and shattered. Magazine pages and recipe cards scattered like frightened bats. Shredded money blossomed from among the wreckage, the remnants of Charlie Argyle's life savings, a pastry shop in Paris that would never be. It billowed toward the sky for a moment before the house imploded altogether, sucking the airborne cash-slaw downward and burying it in the rubble.

An enormous white boulder bounced away from where the kitchen had been, careened off a bathtub, and rolled toward the hole left by the fallen tree.

Helsabeck furrowed his brow. *What was Argyle doing with a big white boulder in his house?*

When Milton saw it crest the edge of the pit above, he recognized it immediately. The sugar boulder he had attempted to bite so many times was about to bite back.

He tried to roll out of the way, but found himself pinned to the ground by the pickax. The tumbling boulder left him no time to do anything but scream. So that's what he did, and with vigor.

The boulder landed directly on top of Milton.

Luckily, that was also where the back end of the pickax's blade protruded. The sugar boulder struck the sharp metal and split cleanly down the middle, the two halves falling to either side.

One half rolled around the chamber and spun to a stop several feet from Benny's bones.

The other half rolled down the tunnel like a dropped quarter, heading right for Chloe.

Chloe's eyes widened. The squampkins would not let her run, and the split boulder's path led directly to her.

Squampkins flung themselves in its path. They were crushed by the dozen under its heavy, sugared edge, screeching and reeking as they died. Chloe pressed against the mat of vines behind her. Dozens more squampkins threw themselves between her and the advancing boulder.

The boulder crushed them like so many grapes, but it was diverted from its path. It brushed Chloe's nose as it rolled past her, wobbled, and then fell with a great crunch onto the handful of squampkins at her feet.

The groaning, crunching, rumbling, roaring, tumbling, shattering, screaming, smashing, and crashing came to a stop. Milton said, "Eep."

Chloe looked up at what remained of the cupola of vines above her. The squampkins above were looking down at her with an expression something like concern. Now that the tunnels seemed

more stable, the squampkins climbed slowly down and returned to their places around her.

Milton walked on shaky legs to the edge of Benny's chamber, where he could see Chloe.

"It worked. We've got a way out," he said, then wrinkled his nose against the stink of crushed-squampkin goo. "And none too soon. Phew."

"They protected me," Chloe said.

"What?" Milton asked.

"The squampkins. The tunnel was caving in and they protected me," she said.

"You're their tear fountain! You're like treasure!" Milton said. "They're hoarding you, keeping you safe."

Chloe noticed for the first time the night sky, visible through the opening ripped in the tunnel roof. It felt like a fist unclenching in her chest. She took a breath.

Milton took a step toward his sister. The hundreds of remaining squampkins turned toward him and hissed. Milton was reminded that the creatures' protection extended only to Chloe.

"Oh," came a sound from behind Milton.

He turned and saw Helsabeck standing at the edge of the pit. Helsabeck's eyes glimmered with tears. Milton followed his gaze.

He was looking at his son's bones.

"Benny," he said softly.

"I'm sorry, Mr. Helsabeck," Milton said, but the man did not seem to have heard him.

"Milton," Chloe said, panic edging back into her voice.

Her brother turned. The squampkins were advancing on him.

"I think my squampkins are upset," she said. The legion of little creatures seethed at Milton, and at the starlit opening newly ripped into the roof of their chamber.

"*Your* squampkins?" Milton asked. At least fifty of the creatures were taking steps toward him, arms raised, sharp little fingernails glinting in the moonlight. Milton took a step back.

"I think," said Chloe, "they're upset that you ripped their roof off."

The squampkin nearest Milton charged, its arms outstretched. Milton leaped backward but his heel caught on the pickax, and he fell onto the bottom he kept padded with candy in case of just such a tumble.

The squampkin threw itself at him and Milton kicked, his toe catching it under the chin and sending it tumbling back on its own vine.

"No!" Chloe shouted, as more squampkins swarmed toward Milton. She tried frantically to think.

Three squampkins were on Milton's legs and climbing fast; he kicked and swatted at them, scrambling backward. "Aagh!" he screamed at the pinch of their strong little hands.

A squampkin leaped onto his left hand and then dug its fingers and toes into the fabric of Milton's jacket, pinning his arm to his side.

"No! No!" Helsabeck was hopping from foot to foot at the edge of the pit, looking down at Milton, helpless.

Chloe looked at the scores of squampkins still watching her. They seemed unconcerned by their siblings trying to tear apart her brother nearby. Milton screamed.

Chloe's eyes fell on the half of the white boulder to her left. An image of more peaceful times flashed in her brain, the memory of reading by sugar-flame light in Argyle's kitchen.

Milton had grabbed the flashlight with his free hand and was beating at the squampkins climbing up his legs and over his belly. A dozen of the things were now on him.

With every blow, the flashlight's beam fell on Chloe, momentarily illuminating the tangle of vines beneath her. With each brief moment of light, she caught another glimpse of the ground between the squampkin vines.

There! Chloe's keen eyes picked out a small white stick with a scarlet head lying on the clay. She crouched, retrieved the match, and struck it against the side of the empty matchbox.

Her brother screamed again. He was completely covered in squampkins. Chloe did not allow herself to look, but, rather, turned and touched the burning match to the sugar boulder.

Jealous hearts do not catch fire so easily or burn so well. The flame barely had to court the sugar before kissing its crystalline white face and creating a ghostly flame that danced between blue and orange, spreading like spilled liquid over the boulder.

Within moments, the tunnel to Chloe's left was ablaze. The smell of caramel and a thick, black smoke filled the space.

She screamed, and hoped the squampkins were as protective of her as they seemed.

Milton could barely hear his sister's scream from beneath the pile of angry squampkins, but he sensed their rage turn to panic.

They had to rescue Chloe from the flames.

The creatures scrambled over one another to get off of Milton, then raced back down the tunnel. *Toffee?* thought Milton, the smell of burnt sugar reaching his nostrils. Even in the horror and chaos of the monsters' tunnel, his stomach had the presence of mind to say growl.

He sat up and saw his sister, carried on a tide of panicked squampkins, rushing over the ground toward him, away from a wall of flames.

Milton barely had time to get to his hands and knees before the wave of creatures overtook him, sweeping him up in their current and carrying him screaming toward the walls of the pit.

Looking behind him, Milton caught just a glimpse of dozens of squampkins, some of them afire, madly flinging dirt onto the blazing half-boulder of sugar. But only a glimpse before he and Chloe were carried up the walls of the tunnel and dropped on the soft earth at the pit's edge.

There was a squeal like a cannon-shot piglet.

Beulah! thought Milton and Chloe.

But no, it was only Helsabeck reacting to the hordes of

squampkins suddenly surrounding him. He dropped his ax, turned, and sprinted toward the wreckage of the Argyle house.

"Milton!" shouted Chloe, as dozens and dozens more squampkins swarmed out of the hole and began dragging her downhill, toward the hole Milton, Helsabeck, and Porifera had earlier dug.

"No!" shouted Milton, grabbing Helsabeck's dropped ax. The squampkins were traveling too fast for Milton to catch up with them. He squinted in the moonlight, trying to pick out those squampkins directly holding Chloe.

Two larger specimens held Chloe's right arm pinned to her side. With his eyes, Milton traced the vines at the base of their spines back to where they crested the edge of the pit.

He leaped forward, ax drawn back over his head, and brought it down hard, severing the two vines. The two creatures at her arm hissed and fell. Chloe gave a short yelp as she fell to the ground, then scrambled to her feet.

Milton swung the ax and severed another vine, then another. Chloe kicked at the creatures around her, freeing her legs. Milton chopped through two more vines at once, then raised the ax and struck another. A half-dozen squampkins were withering and dying at Chloe's feet, thanks to her brother's handy axmanship.

Three squampkins threw themselves at Milton from behind, knocking the ax from his hand.

Chloe grabbed a squampkin tangled in her hair, ripped it loose, and flung it to the ground. She kicked and ripped her way forward through the grasping hands, and was suddenly free. She ran.

As Milton wrenched a squampkin from his shoulder, he saw Chloe crossing the lower patch, heading for the street. He stumbled forward, shaking off the squampkin gripping his shin and running after his sister.

The Nasselrogt children ran for their lives, across the street and toward the avocado house. Behind them, squampkins boiled up from the earth and scrambled after them, their vines dragging behind. Black, burnt-sugar-scented smoke hung in the air.

Chloe hit Helsabeck's door first.

"It's locked!" she cried, as Milton arrived beside her.

The Nasselrogt children turned, their backs to the door. The squampkins had crossed the street and were swarming over Helsabeck's lawn. There was nowhere to run.

"I can't go back underground," Chloe said.

Milton took her hand.

"You won't go anywhere alone," he said.

Crouched in the wreckage of Argyle's house, in a flurry of recipe scraps and money-colored confetti carried on a caramel-scented wind, Helsabeck could not close his eyes without seeing his son's bones against the darkness of his lids. The fear that had so long paralyzed him, and the loneliness he felt for his lost son, finally fermented into a deep and terrible rage.

* * *

Chloe's eyes were closed, her hand clasped tightly in Milton's. The squampkins were a few heartbeats away.

There was a squeal like a cannon-shot piglet.

Milton whooped in giddy hope and Chloe opened her eyes. Never would Milton have believed he could be so relieved at the sight of a school bus.

Beulah had arrived.

The bus rolled over the squampkin vines stretched across the road, the pressure of the heavy tires momentarily stopping the creatures in their tracks.

The bus came to a stop, its wheels straddling the vines.

"Pneumatics!" shouted Chloe.

Milton looked at her, confused, before another brain-hamster jumped on the wheel and he understood.

"Pneumatics!" he shouted.

The school bus door swung open and Beulah leaned from the driver's seat. A Milkhammer, Erica Milkhammer, stood in the seat behind her. Their wide eyes followed the legion of vines trailing underneath the bus, across Helsabeck's lawn, to the spines of the orange creatures advancing on Beulah's favorite minor miners.

The squampkins were only feet from Milton and Chloe.

"Pneumatics!" they shouted together.

Then Beulah understood. She reached for the dashboard, then pushed the large green button.

The bus sighed and, like a big, tired dog, hunkered down onto the ground. The squampkin vines were pinched between the bus's undercarriage and the pavement; they pulled tight, and the squampkins were caught fast.

Legions of tiny orange hands tipped in tiny black nails were arrested. Groping in the air inches from the two Nasselrogt children, the squampkins pulled with all their might against the vines holding them.

A shriek erupted from behind the bus.

"Over there." Erica Milkhammer pointed across the squampkin patch. Beulah turned.

Helsabeck, with a terrible war cry, was charging across the patch with his ax. He skidded to a stop at the edge of the street, a few paces from where the squampkin vines disappeared beneath the bus.

Mr. Helsabeck let the ax get happy. Ignoring the stench and his own exhaustion and fear, he swung the ax down into the vines.

Three of the squampkins swiping at Chloe and Milton crumpled to the ground, collapsing in on themselves.

Helsabeck chopped again and again, chewing steadily through the vines. Black sludge splattered up at him and stuck to the blade, but nothing slowed him down. He waded into the stink, swinging, each chop dropping another few squampkins to rot at the Nasselrogt children's feet.

Within minutes it was over. All of the squampkin vines were cut, and all of the squampkins dead.

Helsabeck stood leaning on the ax, catching his breath. He felt more awake than he had in a year, and smelled worse than he had in his entire life.

The squampkin vines were withering and dying behind him, rot traveling their lengths to where they disappeared into the ground.

Beulah and Erica Milkhammer emerged from the school bus, fleeing the stink of the squampkin goo that was spreading beneath it.

Milton and Chloe stood on the stoop of the avocado house and tried to believe that they had made it through the night alive. Dead, shriveling squampkins littered the lawn before them.

Chloe looked up at the sky. It had never before seemed so wide, nor the moon and stars so wonderful.

There was a rumbling from the squampkin patch. The vines holding up the tunnel walls beneath it were dying, the structure collapsing. Helsabeck could hear their slithering rasp, muffled by the earth. From the front of the Argyle house to the top of the hill on which the box elder had once stood, the patch was collapsing.

Yon Kinsky Kozinsky Porifera's legs vanished into the earth.

The edges of the hole at the base of the fallen tree crumbled inward and buried the bones of Benny Helsabeck.

The ground buckled and puckered. Then the entire yard surrounding the wreckage of the Argyle house sank.

Milton and Chloe still had not let go of each other's hand. What was there to say? Milton leaned toward her.

"Porifera told me . . ." he said, but trailed off, Chloe was staring at the sky.

"Chloe," he said. She turned to look at him.

"Mom and dad are still alive."

Chapter 32

Fell into the Arms

The yellow school bus pushed on through the night, past the prairie where Urchin House stood, and into the dawn.

Milton and Chloe told Beulah their real story, admitting that they were not miners, but runaway minors as she had first suspected. Considering the circumstances, Beulah forgave them. By the end of the ride, there were no more secrets or fibs between them.

They arrived home with the sun. Up and down the street, other children were climbing onto other school buses as Milton and Chloe emerged from their own.

"Mom and Dad will probably be at work," said Milton.

But Chloe shook her head—*no*—and pointed at their house.

In the front window, two familiar figures were staring out from behind the glass. Like Mr. Helsabeck, Milton and Chloe's parents were keeping vigil, hoping against hope that someday their children would return.

Milton and Chloe ran to the door, which had been left unlocked for months now on the chance that these two children would come back and find it open to them.

As the sun rose over the Nasselrogt home, two smaller figures could be seen in the front window, falling into the arms of the parents who were waiting for them.

Epilogue

Mr. Helsabeck hired Brad and Erica Milkhammer to help him clean out Benny's room. Their mother showed up every day at noon with plates of peanut butter-free sandwiches and carrot sticks. By the second week, the cleaning was done. But they had become accustomed to having lunch together, and Margery, sandwiches in hand, continued to bring the twins for visits.

Margery Milkhammer and James Helsabeck got along so well that, one day, Margery sent Brad and Erica out to eat their sandwiches on the front stoop.

There was a red delivery truck parked in front of the remains of the Argyle house across the street. A bald man was standing before it, hands on hips, surveying the wreckage. His grimace revealed golden teeth. The glass of his round spectacles shone in the noonday sun.

This had been one of Gardner Gray's favorite squampkin patches, a healthy crop that could have come back year after year for who knows how long. Now it lay in ruins, and would probably be destroyed completely when the house was demolished and the land cleared.

It was a shame that the man who had planted the patch had been so incompetent a boob. What was his name? It was some kind of sock. . . . Gym? Tube? Bobby?

"Argyle," he said aloud, taking a mental journey to a year earlier, to when he had found Mr. Argyle empty-handed, unable to pay his tithe, and muttering about candy.

It had been a terrible shame to have had to show the man the inside of his red truck. Argyle had been a screamer.

But the secret knowledge of squampkins was too dear to be entrusted to fools. *Who,* he wondered, *had cared for the patch in Argyle's absence?* Gray ran a hand across his bald head and licked his golden teeth.

"Who are you?" Gray turned to find a pair of twins with identical, pinched, possumlike faces looking up at him.

"A friend," said Gray, letting his golden grin spread across his face, "looking for friends."

Brad and Erica squinted against the glare of his teeth.

"Who are your friends?" asked a Milkhammer.

"Whoever tended this patch. You see, I haven't yet met these friends. I only know they could have become very rich had they cared for what they were given."

"Rich?" said a Milkhammer.

"And more," said Gray. "They could have reaped whatever their hearts had the imagination to sow."

The Milkhammers' eyes met.

"I wish dearly that I could find my friends. I owe them . . . so much."

"What if . . ." one Milkhammer began, thinking of all the things the twins could have. "What if we were the ones who took care of the patch?"

"Then you, my dears, would be my friends."

The twins grinned.

"Then we're your friends," said the two Milkhammers. Gray licked his teeth and rubbed his head.

"Step into my truck," he said.

Minutes later, Gardner Gray shut the back door of his truck, climbed into the scarlet cab, and started the motor. He had many more squampkin patches on which to collect before the day's end.

Postscript

PUMPKIN CHOCOLATE-CHIP COOKIES
Recipe by Charles Argyle

In the search for these cookies, Charles Argyle found terrible creatures, madness, and his own death. The recipe can be doubled.

INGREDIENTS
2 C. canned pumpkin
1 1/2 C. light brown sugar
1 t. ground cinnamon
1 t. ground ginger
1 1/2 t. ground cloves
1/2 C. unsalted butter
1/2 C. vegetable shortening
1/2 C. granulated sugar
1 egg
1 egg yolk
1 C. all-purpose flour
1/2 t. baking soda
1/4 t. salt
12 oz. chopped chocolate (or chocolate chips)

First, make the Pumpkin Paste. Combine the canned pumpkin, 1 cup of brown sugar, the cinnamon, ginger, and cloves. Mix well, and spread on a baking sheet. Bake at 300^0 F for one hour, stirring every ten minutes or so, until thick and dark. Cool to room temperature.

Preheat oven to 350^0 F.

In a large bowl, beat the butter, shortening, the remaining 1/2 cup of brown sugar, and 1/2 cup of granulated sugar until light and fluffy. Add the egg and extra egg yolk, and beat well. Add the prepared pumpkin paste and beat well.

In a separate bowl, combine the flour, baking soda, and salt. Stir the flour mixture into the pumpkin mixture, then add the chopped chocolate.

Drop by heaping tablespoonsful onto a greased cookie sheet. Bake seven minutes, until golden brown on the edges. Makes four dozen, and sometimes inspires madness and death.